Breaths of Suspicion

By the same author

Design for Murder
Dead Ringer

The Arnold Landon Novels

Shadowmaker
Dragonhead
Grave Error
Headhunter
The Ways of Death
Dead Secret
An Assumption of Death
The Ghost Dancers
The Shape Shifter
Suddenly as a Shadow
Angel of Death
A Short-Lived Ghost
The Cross Bearer
Bloodeagle
A Wisp of Smoke
The Devil is Dead
Men of Subtle Craft
A Trout in the Milk
Most Cunning Workmen
A Gathering of Ghosts
Goddess of Death

Breaths of Suspicion

ROY LEWIS

ROBERT HALE · LONDON

Robert Hale Limited
Clerkenwell House
Clerkenwell Green
London EC1R 0HT

www.halebooks.com

Typeset in 10½/16 Palatino
Printed in Great Britain by the MPG Books Group,
Bodmin and King's Lynn

PROLOGUE

Looking back, Joe, my boy, I realize I should never have attended that fateful meeting at the Abbey Inn that Sunday.

Not that I really had a great deal of choice. My attendance had been requested by that arch-villain, Lewis Goodman. Since he held a great deal of my paper I knew it would be unwise to refuse to appear. The invitation was more of a demand than a friendly invitation.

Ever since the debacle over the *Running Rein* affair I had been unable to escape Goodman's clutches. He made no great financial demands upon me—because he knew they would hardly be satisfied—and indeed, he refrained from calling in the individual bills when they fell due. In return, of course, he felt able to ask various 'favours' of me . . . and even of these, there had been few.

So, when he called upon me to attend the meeting, I went with trepidation in my heart. I was attending the Assizes at Nottingham at the time so was able to make my reluctant way to the Abbey Inn without difficulty that Sunday. The inn lay at a small distance from the path, among the trees near the main road towards Thoresby. As I approached it I could see it was not a particularly hospitable hostelry: the Abbey Inn had seen better days, when the Plymouth stages had passed by its doors. Now it presented a generally bedraggled appearance, its thatch straggly in places, its windows darkened with smoke and its yard wandered by unhealthy-looking fowl. The doorway was low, and I had to stoop when I entered.

The dark-ceilinged room I walked into was empty apart from the small group of men huddled around a table in the far corner. There was no fire in the grate, but a swirl of greasy smoke hung like a pall below the grimy, blackened beams. I should have left at that moment as the sharp stench of stale beer and ancient gravy caught at my throat, but Lewis Goodman was already rising to his feet to greet me.

He was smiling, but he did not appear well. Some of his confident air seemed to have deserted him since our last meeting and there were sagging strips of flesh below his suspicious eyes.

'James! I'm glad you have made an appearance. Come, join us in our discussion.'

I looked past him to the others present. Jem Saward I already recognized as a fellow member of the Inner Temple: I had seen him hanging around the fringes of the courts, notably at the Old Bailey, though he was not reputed to have established a practice of any consequence. Yet he dressed well enough, and his collars and cuffs were always clean; indeed, he presented a certain dandified appearance. I glanced at him, turned to the second man. It was someone once more I recognized: a disreputable individual called Agar whom I had once—at Goodman's behest—defended. I was not pleased to find myself once more in his company.

The third individual caused me a start of surprise. He was a renowned banker, by the name of Sadleir. We had not been introduced but I knew him by sight as a fellow member of the Reform Club. He sat there stiffly in a black frock coat and light tweed trousers, a gold chain stretched across his vest. He seemed ill at ease in this company; out of place. I had a presentiment of danger. I turned to Goodman. 'You'll forgive me, but I am a busy man and while your invitation to meet you here was pressing, I fear I must ask that you tell me what this is all about.'

Goodman smiled again: his smile always gave me a slight shiver down my back. He glanced at his companions, and winked broadly. 'This is a meeting of a group of investors. I asked you here in order that you should be given the opportunity to make your own investment to match ours.'

I felt like laughing in his face. He knew the state of my finances. My debts were escalating at an alarming rate, in spite of the considerable income I was receiving as a successful Old Bailey barrister but I was in no position to invest in any project—and would have been disinclined in any case, if he was involved. I was about to say something to this effect when a cold draught touched the back of my neck. I turned, looked back.

Standing in the doorway was my arch-enemy, Lord George Bentinck.

He stood there as though rooted. There was malice in every line of his proud, arrogant body. He stared at me coldly. 'I thought I recognized you, James, entering this disreputable hovel. I was intrigued. I wondered—' He paused as his gaze slipped past me to the rest of the company. Slowly, he raised one aristocratic eyebrow. He clearly recognized Goodman, and his handsome lip curled. He looked at the others, silently, took note of the banker, a fellow MP. Then, after several tense moments, he half-turned to leave the room.

Over his shoulder, he said, 'Well, here we have as fine a parcel of scoundrels as ever one could expect to see!'

The door slammed behind him. For a brief time I remained rigid, unable to move. No one spoke but I felt a raging fury stir in my chest. I had no desire to be in this company; Bentinck hated me and would no doubt at some time in the future find good reason to slander me further, and do all he could to blacken my reputation, seeing me in this company. My anger was directed to Goodman for bringing me here, but also towards Bentinck himself, the arrogant, aristocratic humbug, cheat, fraud and hypocrite.

Goodman a laid a hand on my arm, but I flung it off. I almost ran recklessly and there was a scraping of chairs as the others rose to their feet. I rushed to the door, foolishly, thinking there would be some way of challenging Bentinck, persuading him ... but of what?

My action was mindless, careless, but how was I to know that my reaction on that day formed part of events that meant my old enemy had seen his last dawn? For within a matter of twenty minutes my sworn enemy Lord George Bentinck would be stretched lifeless on the edge of the woods—and I would be hurrying back to Nottingham. . . .

But I am getting ahead of myself again. Parliament. You asked me how I had succeeded in my quest for a seat in Parliament, and I promised to tell you. It's a complicated story, full of twists and turns, violence and, yes, death.

And while the Abbey Inn played its part, I need to start before that fateful, and fatal day at the disreputable hostelry near Thoresby. Parliament, ah yes. . . . It would offer me a glittering future, and could be a haven for me, avoiding my creditors and my enemies. . . .

PART ONE

1

Big Ed.

It could have been that, you know, rather than Big Ben. When I was returned on the second occasion, as the Member for Marylebone in the Liberal interest, it was in the company of Sir Benjamin Hall: in fact, the second time I was elected I topped the poll with 5,194 votes as against Ben's total of 4,015. Anyway, Sir Benjamin and I were the two sitting members at Marylebone at the time the great clock was mooted, and if things hadn't gone, shall we say, rather badly for me, with my enemies closing ranks in a concerted attack upon me about that period, Big Ed it could have been, rather than Big Ben.

And Big Ed has a certain *ring* about it, don't you agree? A certain *tone*. Hah! You laughed!

Of course, in those days before I had even met your mother, I wasn't known as Ed, not in England, even within the family: my parents, brothers and sisters, they all referred to me as Edwin. And at the Bar, professional etiquette always demanded the use of my surname, James. Of course, things were different in the more relaxed social atmosphere in the United States later on, where I spent ten years in the legal and newspaper business. I recall that Walt Whitman called me Ed right from the commencement of our acquaintance. As did Mark Twain and Bret Harte, and John C.

Heenan, bareknuckle champion of the world, when I was arranging his fights in the States and Europe.

But in matters of that kind, things were always less socially stiff across the Atlantic.

However, in London it was James at the Bar; or Edwin in the family; or the Honourable Member for Marylebone when I rose to my feet in the House of Commons.

And for a little while, Big-headed Jimmy, or Necessity James (a quip from that snivelling jackanapes, Henry Hawkins, later to become Mr Justice Hawkins: his constant snide comment being *Necessity knows no Law*). But I'll get to that. You've asked me how it was that I came to be elected the Honourable Member for Marylebone.

Edwin James, QC, MP. . . .

I don't recall precisely at what point I set my eyes on election to the House of Commons. I suppose, in a sense, it was a natural ambition. After all, once my father forced me to set aside my leaning towards the footlights (I played in a number of penny gaffs, and even the Theatre Royal in Bath, as a stage-struck young man) and ensured I took up practice at the Bar I felt the need to do well. Thereafter, when I realized I had a talent for the courtroom (which was not unlike a theatre, anyway) ambition drove me to seek high office, if only to prove wrong my father's sneers at my likely professional failure. And to succeed at the Bar and reach the dizzy heights of Lord Chancellor of England it was, of course, necessary to enter into politics. To become Solicitor General or Attorney General demanded a seat in the House, and it did no harm either if one aspired to a judgeship.

Political influence was always a useful shaft in one's quiver. Indeed, a necessary one.

So once I was launched at the Bar, and found myself gathering laurels for my performances in the courtroom, particularly after the *Running Rein* affair, I also set my sights on Parliament. I have to admit, I had no great leanings towards a particular political group. Obviously, the Tory party would be a good bet, for it was in power at the time. It was for that reason that I had first sought membership of the Carlton Club, in the days of the Tory administration of Sir Robert Peel. You'll recall I had been frustrated in that attempt by the blackballing machinations of my enemy, Lord George Bentinck, who had never forgiven me for the manner in which I had attacked him in the hearing arising from the Derby of 1844. Since the Carlton was closed to me, I decided that Reform would become my political mission in life and I cultivated the necessary connections among those who sat on the Whig benches in the Commons. And when I was finally proposed for membership of the Reform Club, no black balls were forthcoming, which had not been the case at the Carlton. The first step had been made: I was mingling with the leading Liberals of the day.

As for Bentinck and the Derby business, of course, as I've already explained to you, I was never able to make public my discoveries concerning the disappearance of *Running Rein*, the winner of the 1844 race. For some time after the affair a fierce fire burned within me, a desire to make further attacks on Lord George Bentinck, to reveal all I knew to the magistrates and recount the whole explosive affair to the newspapers, but I have to admit that the emotion was not of long duration: the fire was damped down by the fact that actual proofs would be almost impossible to obtain; if everything came out my own reputation could be scarred, and in any event I had become very busy, as briefs flooded into my chambers and I began to be seen as a rising star at the Bar.

So I kept my counsel. While Bentinck simmered on the sidelines, nursing his hatred of me.

Talking of my practice, over the course of the next few years after *Running Rein* I gradually abandoned my work in the Bankruptcy Courts, or, at least, I appeared in such causes far less often as other, more remunerative and more attractive opportunities were presented to me. Newspaper reports of my performance in the *Running Rein* case had brought me to the attention of the litigious public as well as the attorneys, and hacks crowded into the courtroom when I appeared, to write up my witty asides in the weekend journals and devote columns to the cross-examinations in which I brought out the more salacious details of life among actresses, aristocrats and members of the flash mob. So, although I was asked from time to time in the clubs to comment on the 1844 Derby affair, I was never able to reveal the entire truth that lay behind the *Running Rein* disappearance, largely because of my indebtedness to that villain, Lewis Goodman. In any event, my practice picked up enormously.

And I have to admit that Goodman himself was behind at least some of my growing success. It was clear to me that many of the clients who came to my chambers arrived there as the result of his recommendations. I would be the last to aver that they were *desirable* clients socially: they counted among their number magsmen and card sharps, insurance fraudsters and night house supporters, pugilists, actresses and clipsmen. But it was all business, and my clerk, Villiers, was kept well occupied. But I also draw attention to the fact that my practice grew not only on the backs of river low-life and acquaintances of Lewis Goodman. The reality was that in those days all levels of society found themselves repairing to the law courts: it was a litigious age. And once it became known among the attorneys that I was a man who could hold his corner, fight a case with vigour and wit and destroy a witness in merciless cross-examination, many of those in high positions in Society beat a path to my door.

And fortunately, the newspapers took note of these sensation cases: *The Times* featured me prominently in its law reports, the *Morning Chronicle* slavered over some of the more intimate details revealed during my cross-examinations in breach of promise cases and I found my growing fame in the courtroom reflected in the number of social invitations I began to receive from members of the Upper Ten Thousand. In short I was beginning to ascend the social ladders, to the wide-eyed surprise of my father, who had never become reconciled to me since my early stated desire to seek my fortune on the stage. His grudging yearly allowance had finally forced me to the more acceptable pursuit of a career at the Bar, but now that I was succeeding, he seemed oddly out of sorts, having predicted from his lofty position as a Secondary of the City of London that he doubted I would ever settle down to hard work.

And it certainly was hard work. I was never a black letter lawyer: I make no secret of the fact that I made much use of penurious devils to raise the salient legal points for me in the more difficult cases, (as that envious toad Sir Henry Hawkins pointed out) but that was par for the course for all who worked at the Bar. Thesiger, Kelly, Wilkins and Cockburn all adopted the same practice as did most men inundated with well-remunerated briefs.

And talking of Alexander Cockburn, a surprising thing happened. In the *Running Rein* case he had been content to make use of his position as senior counsel to fade into the background when the case began to go sour on us, and he had disappeared entirely when the brickbats began to be thrown from the Bench. I was the one who stood up to be bloodied, though in fact the injuries turned out to be superficial in that the diatribes hurled by Baron Alderson actually resulted in an increase of business for me, not least among the racing fraternity, which included, naturally, most of the aristocracy at the time. And, perhaps because I stuck it out manfully, endured the strictures of the Benchers of the Inner Temple and made no complaint, Cockburn's attitude changed towards me. It was in fact he who made the first move, one evening when our paths crossed at the gambling tables in The Casino. He invited me to share a bottle with him; we fell to discussing various matters regarding women, horses and prize fights and the upshot of it was that he invited me back to his chambers where we maintained a convivial conversation over several bottles of port well into the early hours of the morning.

In other words, a sort of friendship arose between us. We shared interests in common. He enjoyed card-playing as a pastime, and he had scrambled out of enough West Country windows in his youth, in avoidance of angry husbands, to be amused by my own predilections in that respect. Mind you, he had a better figure for that kind of escapade: he was far slimmer than my own portly self.

I have no doubt that he was, to some extent, responsible for my easy acceptance into the higher ranges of Society also: the fact he was a companion of mine from time to time at the night houses was noted by the gentry who frequented these locations, and my name began to appear much more frequently alongside his on the guest lists at fashionable houses in Norfolk, Sussex, Yorkshire and even Scotland. I would not go so far as to say that Cockburn and I became boon companions, but during that period we enjoyed each other's company, and this was duly noted among people who mattered.

It was an expensive business, of course, moving into the world of bankers and politicians, aristocrats, admirals and major generals, but the briefs were coming in and I found myself rushing between Exchequer and Old Bailey and Common Pleas, travelling by coach over rutted roads to the Assize Courts on the Home Circuit and acting as junior to some of the more prominent Queen's Counsel in the land. Expensive, yes, but the curious fact was that although that underworld villain, Lewis Goodman, held so much of my paper, and my financial indebtedness to him grew ever larger each year, he made few attempts to dun me . . . in fact, he made none. From time to time he would cancel a debt due, or extend the time limit on a bill for no apparent reason, although there were other occasions when he made use of that indebtedness to put some pressure upon me.

I recall, for instance, that he approached me one night when I was at the tables at one of the night houses he owned in Regent Street. I was reluctant to recognize him, but he stood beside me, tall, elegant, immaculately attired, gravely observing the play for a little while before turning to me and murmuring softly, 'A word, if I may, Mr James?'

I hesitated, reluctant to be observed in his company, but it was an opportune moment to leave the table for I was losing heavily, as usual, so after a moment's delay I followed his slim form towards a far corner of the crowded room. A table stood there, empty apart from a bottle of claret and two glasses. Goodman flicked up his coat tails, seated himself and gestured to the vacant seat beside him. I glanced around: the bulky form of Porky Clark hovered nearby. The scar-faced ex-pugilist was never far from his master, like a protective bulldog. I took the proffered seat reluctantly, as Lewis Goodman poured two glasses of claret, his lean, delicate fingers almost caressing the glasses.

'To your continuing professional health, Mr James,' he murmured, raising his glass.

It was a toast I could hardly refuse since so much depended on it.

'It seems you are doing very well these days,' Goodman continued, his gleaming eyes fixed on me and a slight smile playing on his sensuous lips. 'I follow the law reports in the newspapers with much interest in view of your forensic exploits.'

I made no reply, still unhappy at the thought of being observed in the company of such a notorious villain.

'And the Society papers too,' he added. 'Fashionable houses, balls, the attention of high-born ladies of light temperament, no doubt . . .'

'What do you want, Goodman?' I demanded irritably. 'I'm aware there are some bills falling due next week, but I assure you—'

He chuckled. He raised a hand, and I caught the glint of gold at his wrist. He was always expensively dressed, this prominent member of the flash mob, and was known for his propensity to sport considerable jewellery about his person: gold wristbands, diamond tiepins, ruby rings on his left hand. I always considered it pretentious, and low, to demonstrate his wealth in such an obvious manner. 'Please, Mr James, let's not consider the question of the bills falling due. I'm aware that a gentleman of your standing, and future prospects, must lay out a considerable amount of tin to further his career. Holding your paper is, as you are well aware, a sort of insurance for me, rather than a way of becoming rich. And, I'm sure you'll agree, I've been of an obliging nature in the matter of timely repayment.'

I knew what he meant by insurance, recalling the murder that had followed the *Running Rein* affair. Reluctantly, I nodded agreement, and sipped the claret he had provided. It was of an excellent vintage, but that did not surprise me. Lewis Goodman was known to live well.

The night house owner sent an appreciative glance around the room, his dark eyes expressing satisfaction. But I was aware that those eyes could also become heavy-lidded with menace, and his handsome, smiling features could mask a deadly intent. 'In fact,' he murmured, 'I have it in mind to cancel the particular bills you refer to. In exchange for a certain favour from you.' His eyes switched to mine, holding my gaze directly. 'The cancellation will not affect your fee-earning capacity, of course.'

I blinked. A knot of suspicion formed in my chest. 'A favour?'

'A certain friend of mine finds himself in a degree of difficulty. He will be appearing at the Old Bailey within the week. I'd like you to represent him.'

I frowned. 'That's not the way things are done, and you know it. I cannot have truck directly with the public like this: a brief must come from an attorney—'

Goodman waved my comment aside with a contemptuous and peremptory flick of the wrist. 'Ha, don't be concerned, the formalities will be attended to. A certain Mr Fryer will be presenting himself at your chamber. He is a respected attorney.'

'As your friend is not?' I ventured. 'Respected, I mean.'

Something glinted in Goodman's eyes but he said nothing for a moment. Then he smiled. 'Let me put the matter in this way. A Mr Edward Agar will be appearing in court on a charge of handling forged papers. Evidence will be presented by Inspector Redwood, an officer of whom you have already some acquaintance, I believe.'

I made no reply, but the old image flashed before my eyes again, of the drowned mistress of Lester Grenwood being dragged from the filthy water of the Thames, under the watchful eye of Inspector Redwood.

'The charge against Mr Agar is a serious one. It will carry a heavy prison sentence, if proved. But it is not in my best interests at this time that Mr Agar should be locked up for the immediate future. It is important to me that he should escape the charge. We have . . . ah . . . certain common interests that need to be promoted.'

Nefarious, no doubt, I thought. 'If I were to act in his defence there would be no guarantee of success,' I warned. 'I can only handle the evidence that is presented and—'

'The evidence is trumped up,' Goodman intervened. 'Inspector Redwood has been after Mr Agar for some time. Agar would never be so foolish as to carry forged papers on his person, in the street.'

'He was apprehended—'

'In broad daylight, on Red Lion Street. The papers were produced from his pockets at Bow Street Police Station. They'd have been planted there.'

'By Inspector Redwood?' I asked in surprise.

'By one of his minions,' Goodman replied.

'I can hardly believe—'

'Believe it!' Goodman snapped. 'And do not affect such a surprised tone. You know as well as I that the blues are as open to corruption as those whom they seek to put away in the hulks.'

I was silent for a little while, aware of the truth of what he was saying. I knew for a fact that Goodman had access even to the Commissioner of Police, if he chose to use his influence. I wondered why he did not use that influence in this instance, but concluded that the situation might be too tricky for that, if it were to be a matter of police corruption. Slowly, I shook my head. 'Even so, I will be able to proceed only on the basis of evidence available to the court. To suggest police corruption—'

'Not to *suggest* it, Mr James. You will prove it.'

'In what manner?' I demanded.

There was an element of wolfishness in Goodman's smile as he regarded me. 'I will provide sufficient evidence, through the medium of the attorney Fryer. All you have to do is present it, and use it to tear the chief witness against Mr Agar to shreds.'

'Redwood?' I doubted.

Goodman shook his head. 'Not Redwood. The arresting officer reporting to him. Police Constable McCarthy.'

And a few days later, when Mr Fryer came to my chambers and presented me with the brief I realized why Goodman wanted me to use the evidence provided. Any other barrister would have been reluctant to use it. It averred that Constable McCarthy was an inveterate gambler, a frequenter of whore houses where he failed to pay the relevant fees, a formerly indigent Irishman corrupted by his environment, all backed by suggestion, innuendo and some witnesses who were prepared to swear to the most unlikely events taking place in the dark streets of the metropolis.

I recall stating to the attorney Fryer in my chambers that if these witnesses were to present their evidence they themselves, by their own admissions, would be open thereafter to criminal charges, as conspirators, pimps and fraudsters. His only reply was that these individuals well understood the consequences. Which meant that Goodman had them in thrall, and they deemed it more discreet to accept such dangers than to deny Goodman the requests he had made of them. Worse could happen to them on the streets of London.

Of course, at the time I was not aware, indeed could not possibly know just how important Edward Agar, the man in the dock, was to Lewis Goodman. I found out later, as I'll explain to you in due course, but for the moment suffice to say that I finally agreed to take the brief, use my best forensic skills to thrash the unfortunate Constable McCarthy, and leave the witnesses, false as they were, to their own individual fates. And that was what happened. At the hearing at the Central Criminal Court I persuaded the jury that the charges against Agar had been trumped up by the unreliable and corrupt Constable McCarthy, and I received prompt payment of a generous fee by way of the attorney Fryer. And two hefty bills of exchange held by Goodman in my name were cancelled.

But I also incurred the enmity of my old acquaintance, Inspector Redwood.

However, it would be a mistake on your part to assume that I was in complete thrall to Lewis Goodman, or that my practice grew only on the backs of such unsavoury clients. Once briefed, a barrister must hold and certainly not express any personal views as to the guilt of his client. He is the mouthpiece of the man he represents, his duty is to do his best to obtain an acquittal, and take the best interests of his client to heart. Of course, I suspected that the evidence dredged up by Goodman against the policeman was of doubtful provenance, and that the witnesses against him were lying through their teeth. And the fact that the proofs given by those witnesses were self-incriminatory was none of my business.

I was performing my duty fearlessly and effectively like any upright member of the Bar.

Inspector Redwood was not of that opinion: he met me after the hearing, as I crossed the wood-blocked street outside the Old Bailey. He raised one hand to his black-varnished top hat, greeting me. His lean, saturnine features were sober, and there was a hard look in his eyes. He fiddled with the shiny buttons on his blue frock coat as he barred my way, standing on the edge of the pavement. That was a habit of the police, you know—they always walked on the pavement edge to avoid the slops that were often thrown down upon their heads.

'My compliments, Mr James. Edward Agar goes free.'

'You failed to make your case.' I made to move past him but he had the temerity to hold me by the shoulder.

'Constable McCarthy is finished in the force now,' he said. 'He has a wife and two children to support—'

'That's not my affair.'

'And those three witnesses you brought into court to destroy his credibility, they've been taken into charge. Will you be defending them, sir?'

'I doubt it.'

Inspector Redwood was silent for a few moments, regarding me owlishly as he stroked his luxuriant sideburns. 'You've been got at, haven't you, Mr James?'

I stood my ground, and stared him out. 'Was Edward Agar *really* carrying forged notes on his person when he was arrested on Red Lion Street?'

'Agar is someone we've been interested in for a long time,' Redwood replied, colouring slightly. 'He's escaped us on numerous occasions, but we'll get him yet.'

'On planted evidence?'

I waited, and Redwood held my glance for several seconds. Then he shook his head, with an air of sadness. 'You're a rising man, Mr James. You should choose your cases with care. You'd be well advised to stay away from the likes of Agar, and the men who back them.'

I was offended by his presumption in giving me advice. But he did not know that it was fully my attention to avoid such contacts. And as I've already intimated to you, my practice was growing not simply on the back of members of the flash mob. I was acting for, and against members of other levels of society.

Such as Lord Huntingtower.

And that gave rise to other problems. Much as I detested Lord George Bentinck for his deviousness, chicanery and double-dealing at the Turf I had to admit he knew his horses. He kept a formidable stable even though his father disapproved: he used various aliases under which he ran his nags. And he spent, and won, immense sums on the races at York and Doncaster and Epsom.

He was what the Spanish called an *aficionado* and was an expert in horseflesh.

This was not something one could say about Lord Huntingtower. Like Lord George he frequented the Turf, spent vast amounts of money and blazoned his skills and knowledge about the courses. But unlike Lord George he did not know his horse-flesh. He was a pompous, braying fool who understood little of breeding and bloodstock, much as he affected to be an expert. And the inevitable result of his ignorance was that he finally found it necessary to cover up his huge losses by fraud.

Which led to his court appearance, and my subjecting him to a sarcastic cross-examination.

The Times loved it. Over the course of three days they devoted five columns to my excoriation of the witness, a butterfly strug-gling under my pin. I exposed his ignorance, his foolishness, his *braggadocio*, and his fraudulent behaviour. On the second day, Lord George himself took a seat in court, in his self-styled role as Protector of the Sport of Kings, but his brow was furrowed, his features dark as he watched Huntingtower wriggling in the witness box. I knew what he was thinking: he hated to see a member of his own class being shamed in this manner, and I suppose I took an extra pleasure in extending the agony, if only to get back at Bentinck for his own behaviour towards me. Lord Huntingtower stood there, elegantly apparelled, smoothly coiffured, disdainful at first behind his luxuriant moustaches and self-confident in his superiority, but as I stripped away the mask, bringing out the low company he kept, the frauds he perpetrated, the sheer ignorance he displayed of the sport at which he professed to be expert, the man seemed to shrivel, hunch in distress as the laughter ran around the courtroom. Bentinck, all the while, glowered at the exhibition, furious at the manner in which I was shredding one of his own class.

But enough of Huntingtower. I mention the matter only to emphasize that my cases were not simply those low-life clients Lewis Goodman eased my way. And oddly enough, my treatment of Lord Huntingtower did nothing to cause the invitations from Society to dry up. I had evidence that the enmity of Lord George Bentinck had further increased towards me as a result of my treatment of Huntingtower, but I cared little for that. The coverage of the Huntingtower trial was satisfying: my name was writ large in the gossip columns; my star was beginning to shine and glitter in a manner that astonished my father.

Running Rein had forced my name before the public; Huntingtower had confirmed my reputation. There were those, like the leader writer in *The Times*, who had already begun to sneer that I was making my reputation in cases that involved merely actresses or horses, but I could afford to ignore such slurs.

I had arrived at the first port of call: henceforth, I knew, my voyage would be even more glittering. The fruits of success were already discernible, and would soon be within my reach.

Which reminds me, I've digressed again, my boy; we were talking of my entry into politics, weren't we?

Well, I first edged into that lime-lighted part of the stage as a result of election committees. And there was also a little additional push as a result of my reluctant connection with that villain, Lewis Goodman. . . .

2

Election committees. One of the most lucrative activities for the Bar was the inevitable bloodletting that always occurred in the aftermath of elections to the House of Commons. The losers at the hustings constantly sought to overturn the result of the ballot and their accusations of bribery and corruption were heard before election committees sitting in the House of Commons. The elections of 1848 were to prove no exception in that regard.

My success in the Bankruptcy Court and in the more aggressive area of the Old Bailey had impressed numerous attorneys but I doubt whether I would have been able to enter the remunerative field of election committee work had it not been for the excessive rush of petitions that emerged in that year, and the effective retirement of Alexander Cockburn from the battlegrounds of the election committee rooms. At that time Cockburn held the lead in election committee work along with Thesiger and Austin but in 1848 Cockburn had disqualified himself from the work by getting elected himself, as MP for Southampton. Thesiger also was forced to decline election briefs when he became Attorney General, and as for Austin, well, he just faded away fatly to a magistracy in the wilds of Hampshire where he made himself unpopular and incurred the enmity of the local squirearchy by refusing to taking poaching seriously.

So I suddenly found myself approached by Mr Coppock, the parliamentary agent. As you might guess, I seized the opportunity with an eager grasp.

In truth, the business suited me perfectly: all elections in those days were tarred with corruption. Local voters needed to be persuaded, and that meant *treating*: riotous nights in the ale houses, seats at boxes in London theatres, a bit of business for a shopkeeper, open house for voters at a local hostelry, the provision of available doxies and the surreptitious transfer of a few golden guineas into individual voting pockets. . . . So you could imagine how enthusiastically and colourfully I exposed these ignoble actions in the hearing of the petitions.

And I was good at it; no, I do not flatter myself when I say I was soon recognized as the best. As a matter of fact, I was presented only last week with a proof copy of Ballantine's *Experiences*. This is what he had to say about my work on election committees: 'Edwin James possessed all the qualities necessary for the work. He had great readiness, handled his facts amusingly but with considerable force, and was never tedious. He was an excellent *Nisi Prius* leader and although not possessed of any remarkable knowledge of the law or profound scholarship, contrived to manage Lord Campbell better than any of his rivals at the Bar.'

And that from someone with whom I had no friendly acquaintance: we disliked each other heartily.

So, as I say, I made a great success at the Lancaster committee hearing, and there quickly followed, as I recall, Carlisle, Bewdley, Norwich and Lincoln. The longest runner was Aylesbury and I tell you, I never worked so hard in my life, scurrying from committee room to committee room, handling as many as four petitions at a time as well as picking up further briefs at *Nisi Prius*. And a few years later, after the 1852 election I took seven petitions in March alone, five more in April and through May and June I was dashing from assize hearings to deal with petitions at Harwich, Plymouth,

Cork, Liverpool and Peterborough. *The New York Times* hit it right on the head when, some years later, it wrote, 'No member or petitioner deemed his chances secure until Mr James had been retained.'

Glory days, my boy, and remunerative!

Yet there was another advantage: work at the election committees extended the range of one's influential acquaintances: very soon I was being invited to weekends at the country house retreats of the great. The Duke of Norfolk, Sir James Duke, the Earl of Yarborough, Sir John Jervis offered me their hospitality; the one-armed hero of the Peninsular War, Lord Raglan, entertained me, as did Lord Combermere, whom Wellington called 'a damned fool' and really was one. Lord Lucan and Lord Cardigan felt the lash of my tongue in court actions but still issued invitations, and I found myself regularly seated for dinner among the leading politicians of the day, including Lord John Russell, Lord Dacre and Viscount Palmerston himself, of course.

So there I was in the late 1840s, still a junior member of the bar, but making more than five thousand a year. I was asking a hundred guineas as a brief fee, and when I attended the assizes at York or Newcastle I called for a further hundred as a retainer. My clerk, Villiers, was kept busy bringing the money in.

Trouble was, I didn't seem to be *seeing* much of it.

The fact is, it's a great thing to dine with high society, but it's also an expensive business. To become a social lion is grand, but it's also costly: clothes, carriages, the need to visit casinos, gambling clubs, demonstrate bravery in placing a bet and careless indifference when losing badly. But I sailed along happily on a sea of witticisms, *bon mots*, anecdotes from the courts and gay expenditure at the tables.

Which was where my next, unexpected stroke of luck came forth. Unfortunately, once again, from the hands of Lewis Goodman.

After the Derby fiasco I had not seen him for some time: I made certain payments to him when my debts grew embarrassingly high but that meant no personal appearance before him. That was the way I preferred things. So when I saw Porky Clark making his way towards me across the crowded floor of the casino that particular evening, I groaned: I guessed it could mean an unpleasant interview. In fact, there was no sign of Goodman himself, and Porky contented himself by handing me a slip of paper.

It was a succinct note.

'My Dear James,

I would consider it a favour if you were able to assist me in looking after one of our clients this evening. He is winning considerably at rouge et noir, *but is somewhat affected by wine. If anything should happen to him, scandal could affect the club. Can you arrange to accompany him to his carriage as early as possible? I note that you have a bill due for payment on Monday. In return for this assistance, I would deem it paid.*

Sincerely,
Lewis Goodman'

A shiver of anticipation ran down my back. The night house owner would not enjoy the run of luck his client was having but I knew what was really bothering Goodman: he owned a range of night houses in the West End and he could suffer badly if a scandal involving a young aristocrat emerged.

I glanced across the room. Porky Clark, standing beside me, touched my arm and gestured towards a particular table. It was surrounded by a group of men, watching the obviously extraordinary run of success being enjoyed by a tousle-haired young buck. He was seated at the tables now, flushed, excited, and clearly on an extended winning run. His dark, curly hair was damp, his eyes sparkling with drink and his hands trembled with inebriated excitement as he gathered in his chips. It would not be easy to winch him away from the scene of his continuing success but as I moved closer towards the table I realized why Goodman was particularly concerned. It wasn't just the money. I looked at Porky Clark, and nodded. Saving this young man from making a fool of himself had two advantages: it would cancel one of my debts to Goodman, but even more important, it would perhaps place me in the good books of his father, whom I had met only twice in the Reform Club. Nodding terms only. Perhaps that situation could improve.

For the young man playing recklessly at *rouge et noir* was the son of the Attorney General of England.

I did not know young Jervis well, though I had met him on a few occasions at Westminster Hall, and he was a member of my own Inn, the Inner Temple. Now, I walked casually across the room and edged my way into the gathering, until I stood behind the Attorney General's son. He was playing wildly, and yet his recklessness was paying off and he was well ahead of the table. He was also drunk. I leaned over him and offered my advice. He turned his head and grinned at me.

'Stop while I'm ahead?' he laughed. 'It's my lucky night!'

I wasn't quite sure that he recognized me and there was little I could do to dissuade him on his current successful play. So I stepped back and waited. He soon began to find that his luck was changing: he still won occasionally, but there were losses too. He was nevertheless well ahead up to the point that the dealer was changed. I watched the changeover: it had significance, I was certain. Goodman would have ordered the replacement: the new dealer, a lean, dark-eyed, cold-featured man with long, predatory fingers would have more control over events. There would now be discreet cheating in the wind.

'Time to leave now,' I whispered in Jervis's ear. 'I know this new man. You'll see a change in your luck, believe me.'

The young barrister leaned back in his seat. Some of the sense behind what I was saying filtered through his drink-sodden mind. With more control than I had ever managed to achieve myself when at the tables, he contemplated the green baize before him in silence, glowered, then almost dazedly collected his chips. He rose to his feet, staggering slightly. He stared at me, and recognition now glimmered in his eyes. 'James. . . .'

'Come. I'll give you a hand, see you to a cab,' I offered.

I collected our capes and canes and assisted young Jervis towards the doors.

The night house owned by Goodman lay in a side lane just off the Strand. When we lurched out into the shuttered street outside all was dark except for occasional gleams of light filtering from closed casement windows in the mean houses nearby. Wisps of cold fog drifted at head height, blurring the eyes with a sharp pungency, a real London Particular if you know what I mean. At two in the morning the cold had a cutting edge to it, seeming to slice into the bones. Young Jervis was now leaning heavily on my arm as I looked around for a waiting hansom cab. He was very drunk and the cold night air seemed to have hit him almost like a blow to the skull.

The doors to the night house closed behind us with a solid thud and we found ourselves isolated in the darkened street.

Unusually, there was no cabman plying for hire to be seen on the dimly lit cobbles. But I guessed if we made our way along the greasy stones towards the main thoroughfare that dimly beckoned to us some fifty yards distant we would soon find a conveyance to take us to my chambers, or those of my companion, whom I recalled vaguely as being lodged near to the Inner Temple.

We staggered forward, Jervis's arm firmly lodged in mine, and I cursed Lewis Goodman roundly under my breath: this was not the manner in which I was accustomed to ending my nights on the town. Additionally, this evening there was a certain complaisant lady, neglected wife of a laudanum-addicted baronet, waiting expectantly in St John's Wood . . . but she would have to wait. At least looking after Jervis would serve to cancel a pecuniary trans-action with the night club owner. . . .

We were some twenty yards from the corner that debouched into the main thoroughfare of the Strand when they materialized out of the haziness of the fog. There were three of them, broad-shouldered, flat-capped, hulking apparitions, armed with cudgels. They emerged from a side alley and were making their way directly towards us but their approach was neither hesitant nor indeterminate: I instantly realized that we were targets. Whether they had been lying in wait for specific individuals emerging from the night house, or we simply happened to be in the wrong place at the wrong time I had no opportunity to determine.

You, my boy, as a man of the sea, you will have knowledge of dockside brawls, no doubt, and your mother has often told me you do not lack bravery. But as for me, well, I have no hesitation in confirming that I had never been over-endowed with physical courage, and I must admit that my first inclination at a possible confrontation was always to turn and run, but my companion's arm was still linked with mine and he chose this inopportune moment to gently slide towards the cobbles, sighing deeply, clearly dizzy, finally overcome by the night air, and befuddled with drink. As the thugs advanced on us I tried desperately to drag Jervis to his feet, turn with me and run back to hammer at the closed doors of the night house we had just left but he complained drunkenly and incoherently, clinging to my arm like a dead weight as the three villains grew closer. I caught a glimpse of raised cudgels and knew we were done for: the area was well known for being haunted by garrotters and I feared the worst. I struggled to release myself from young Jervis's grip so I could take to my heels and leave him to his fate but he hung on tightly in his drunken stubbornness and his weight brought me down with him so that I myself stumbled to my knees. In panic I raised my free arm instinctively to protect my head. There was a swishing sound, and I felt a sharp pain on my forearm, but it was a glancing blow, merely. There would be further blows, I knew, and more crushing. I was on my knees, and John Jervis was huddled against me, helplessly, grunting out the garbled words of some obscene drinking song. There was a stamping of feet, a whirling of bodies, and I heard the clashing of cudgels but amazingly I felt no more blows raining down upon me.

Scraping and stamping and shouting and swearing, heavy breathing, hobnailed boots striking sparks on the cobbled road: I felt I was in the middle of some crazed whirligig and a heavy body suddenly thudded into me, knocked me sideways and then rolled beside me on the cobbles before rising hurriedly again, scrambling back into the darkness behind him. A confused shouting still whirled around me; there was the stink of sweat in my nostrils and I lowered my protective arm, looked fearfully about me to make out bodies closely locked, struggling in some kind of stamping, macabre dance in the drifting fog. A further clashing of cudgels, and a stray heavy boot thudded into my ribs, but I got the impression it was a wayward blow, not even directed towards me. But it slammed the breath out of my lungs and I sank down again, winded. I still feared the worst. But there were no more blows, I heard the clattering of running feet, caught a glimpse of vague outlines fading into the wisps of fog and then a sudden silence, broken only by the harsh breathing of a single individual, half-seen, wide-shouldered, shaven-headed, heavy and almost ungainly, looming over me in the darkness.

'Mr James . . . are you all right?'

Thick gnarled fingers closed on my arm, hauling me to my staggering feet until I was clasped to a broad chest. The heavy features of my rescuer were thrust into mine and I smelled onions and beer on his breath. Satisfied that I was not seriously hurt, my rescuer turned away and hauled to his legs the muttering drunkard at my feet. When he leaned young Jervis into my grasp, it was only then that I recognized our saviour. It was the pugilist, well known as Lewis Goodman's fixer: Porky Clark.

The scarred, battered features were thrust close into mine again, as though he was reassuring himself I was not badly hurt. He began to brush me down, removing dirt from my shoulders and chest, then, after a moment, he nodded satisfaction and let out a gusty, beer-and-pie flavoured breath. 'Mr Goodman don't like trouble so close to his place,' he muttered.

'Where . . . where did they come from?' I asked shakily.

'Them pack rats? There's an alley back of the night house,' Porky replied, nodding in the general direction of Goodman's premises. 'It's happened afore. The villains will've been watching for gennlemen like yous coming out with full pockets.'

'And where did you come from?' I wondered.

He hesitated. The question seemed to bewilder him for a few moments. He scratched his stubbly chin, picked up the battered billycock hat he seemed to have mislaid during the scrimmage with the three thugs and ran a hand over his shaven head. 'Came out afore you, Mr James. Just to take a look around, like.'

There was something unconvincing in his brief explanation, but I thrust the thought aside. I took a deep breath, caressed my injured rib with a gentle hand and swore. 'It's as well you came out too, Porky, or we'd have been well and truly turned over.'

'They was just amatoors,' he opined, grandly boastful. 'They was 'specting easy targets. I put the boot into them. Come on, Mr James, let's get you and Mr Jervis to the Strand. There'll be hansoms there. We'll get you and the young 'onnerble home straightaway.'

He was right. As soon as we emerged stumbling from the dark side street we saw a cab standing there, almost as if it had been waiting for us. Porky Clark raised a hand to the driver, then half-lifted young Jervis inside where he collapsed on the horse-hair seat like a bundle of old clothes. Porky stepped back as I ascended, clutching my sore rib.

'Best not tell Mr Goodman about this,' he muttered. 'He don't like his gennlemen bein' took after they leave the house.'

It would have been the reason Porky had come out into the street before we emerged, I had no doubt. He would be well aware of the dangers that the streets outside the night house might offer to the unwary. He closed the door behind me, and instructed the driver. 'Inner Temple.'

There was the crack of a whip, the cab lurched on its way and Porky Clark was lost once more in the enveloping darkness of the side street.

Beside me, young Jervis was leaning his curly-locked head on my shoulder, and he had begun to snore. I guessed that later that morning he would have little recollection, if any, of the encounter in the alley. He would certainly not be aware that Porky Clark had come to our rescue. I slipped my hand into the pocket of his coat: his purse was still stowed safely there, and it felt comfortably swollen with the night's winnings. I found my fingers itching with a momentary temptation: by extracting a few notes I could make up for some of my own losses that evening, and I had, after all, provided a service to the young rascal. But I resisted the temptation.

It would hardly be wise to relieve the son of the Attorney General of some of his winnings at *rouge et noir*. There was a line that had to be drawn. . . .

So we rattled through the darkened streets to the Inner Temple, and after depositing him at his lodgings I made my way by cab to my assignation in St John's Wood. The lady in question squealed at my dishevelled state and caressed my sore rib tenderly after I explained my heroics of the evening. She was also tenderly acquiescent when I identified other areas of my anatomy that urgently required her soothing attention. . . .

I felt appreciated and not a little proud of my bold activities of the evening.

3

As I've already explained, my adventures in the courtrooms had given me a certain notoriety that was awarded by social lionizing. At that particular time I had been the subject of numerous dinner invitations by notable members of society. A week or so after the incident at Goodman's night house in the Strand I received an invitation to a Friday to Monday occasion at the seat of the Earl of Yarborough, in Norfolk. I was delighted to receive the invitation, though not surprised, because I had recently had occasion to act for him in a rather unpleasant forgery case: he had been pleased with the result and when I met him later by chance, at The Casino, when he was somewhat in his cups, he had issued the invitation. It meant a certain amount of expense for me: a hired carriage to convey me into Norfolk, new clothes, an attendant temporary servant, but it was too important an invitation to back away from. Such invitations from people in High Society could be as rare as bustards in Norfolk for someone who was just reaching the lower rungs of the social scene, as I was at that time.

And the company was certainly glittering that evening: Lady Beauvale, Attorney General Sir John Jervis, Lady Clanricarde, Viscount Palmerston, Sir Charles Greville (along for the gossip, I had no doubt), Captain Gronow, Lord Esher, my learned friend Alexander Cockburn and others whose names have faded in my memory. Oh, yes, I was in exalted company.

It was before dinner on the first evening that Sir John Jervis caught my eye, and motioned to me to stand aside with him near the windows. We stood side by side, each with a glass of Marsala in hand, and admired the view of the sloping lawns in the fading light. But the Attorney General clearly had something on his mind and after very little prevarication Sir John turned to me and smiled. 'Certain rumours have been rippling around the Temple.'

'When have there not, Sir John?' I queried, shrugging.

'This particular rumour concerns a member of my family,' the Attorney General observed. 'It seems there was some kind of fracas in which he became involved . . . after an evening at the card tables. My son has no great recollection of the details, it seems, but I have it on good authority that he escaped a beating, and robbery, as a result of your personal intervention. I am told that you yourself have made no reference to this event, but nevertheless the story has got out. Three thugs set upon you, I am told . . . and there was some injury to yourself.'

I touched my rib, which was still sore and shook my head, pouting slightly in a deprecating fashion. Whoever had been telling the tale seemed to have made no reference to the part played by Porky Clark.

Sir John Jervis regarded me keenly for a few moments. 'I have not yet had the occasion to thank you personally for the assistance you rendered my son John on that evening.'

'It was a matter of chance,' I protested, though as you can imagine, not too vehemently.

'Nevertheless, if you had not been in the vicinity there could have been serious consequences.'

He was silent for a few moments. Sir John Jervis had a somewhat gentle demeanour for a lawyer and successful Parliamentarian. He had a high, pale forehead, dark greying hair receding towards the crown. His eyes were brown, and warm. His face was long, his features regular and he seemed to exude an air of quiet friendliness. He was highly regarded in Government for his sincerity and straight dealing. He had a reputation for honesty. On the other hand he never seemed to be entirely in good health: he suffered much from asthma, you know. It killed him in the end, at a relatively young age, too. But as we stood by the window looking out over the rolling Yarborough estates he was observing me sideways with a kindly glance. 'I hear that your practice grows apace.'

'I am indeed being kept busy,' I murmured. 'I keep a toehold in the Bankruptcy Courts, but other briefs have recently been coming in and I spend a deal of time in the Old Bailey.'

Sir John sucked thoughtfully at his teeth. 'So I understand. And I gather you are interested in the matter of Reform.'

I took a deep breath. 'That is so, Sir John.'

He frowned slightly, thoughtfully. 'I believe you are recently a member of the Reform Club.' He sipped at his Marsala. 'This is not the occasion when one should discuss matters of business, but I wonder whether you would find it convenient to dine with me on Thursday next at the club?'

I was quick to assent, even though I knew it would mean a hasty retreat from Guildford Assizes where I was to be engaged with a breach of promise action that day.

Jervis smiled pleasantly. 'Ha. Good. We'll leave further discussion of the proposition I wish to make to you until then. Meanwhile, we'll say no more. . . . Here are the ladies. We must make ourselves available.'

In they were sailing, the first wave bearing Lady Beauvale and Lady Yarborough, the bosomy Lady Dacre just behind them. And a moment later, to my amazement, I realized that among those ladies who followed there was an old acquaintance.

Marianne Hilliard, formerly Miss Edge, the Sheffield banker's daughter.

It was several years since I had last set eyes on her. My brother

Henry, who now had a medical practice in Harley Street, had met her from time to time in some professional matter or another. Henry, by the way, is the only member of my family who remains in touch with me now I am reduced to penury, even though two others have made their way in the Law, albeit not with such distinction as I. But that is beside the point.

When Marianne caught sight of me her eyebrows rose, and she smiled. Brother Henry had told me that since her marriage to that fool Crosier Hilliard, she had given birth to two children. The *accouchements* had done little to affect her attractiveness: her waist had thickened a little, no doubt, but her bosom had become even more magnificent and there was a new assurance in the tilt of her head . . . even though, as I recalled, she had never been lacking in the matter of self-assurance. She was wearing a cream gown that set off her shoulders impressively, a hint of lace maintaining the proprieties at the shadow between her breasts, and when she looked at me I detected the light of surprise, followed by a certain sparkle of pleasure in her eyes that made me feel . . . prospects?

I often had that almost instant effect on women, you know, even if I did look like a prize-fighter. Or perhaps it was because I had that rugged appearance. A lived-in face.

The swirl of the gathering meant that for the moment we were unable to have anything other than a brief acknowledgement and a polite query as to family. I cast my eyes around the room when she made only an offhand reference to her Hussar husband. He was not present. I was then engaged in conversations with Lady Beauvale and her group: it seemed they had been following my recent progress in the courts with some attention. The law courts were always a great attraction for the ladies in high society, you know, particularly where the hearing concerned some of their own and involved scandalous behaviour, such as rocking gondolas, rustling skirts, private detectives hiding behind curtains and the evidence of servants observing events through bedroom keyholes.

If ladies carried enough influence they could manage to obtain an invitation to sit on the bench beside the judges and follow matters at first hand. There would be much fluttering of fans and the occasional fainting fit when scurrilously sexual behaviour was exposed, and proceedings were often halted while a lady was assisted from the courtroom, overcome by her corsets and the sinful revelations from the witness box. Most managed to stick things out, however, and come back next day for more discussions of keyholes, and stained sheets and unusual sexual positions. And since many of the briefs that were now falling into my hands concerned breach of promise, criminal conversation or liaisons between actresses and sons of peers, you can imagine that I was quickly surrounded and detained by the female set, eager for salacious gossip.

Cockburn, I noticed, was in similar demand that evening. But then, he was always known to be a ladies' man. And it was rumoured that he had fathered two children by a butcher's wife in Cambridge. Such gossip was a matter for shivery attraction to the ladies.

Then there were introductions to other members of the party, a period listening to the sharp gossip of Greville on political rivals and a kindly word from our host, Lord Yarborough. It was, incidentally, on that occasion that I was introduced for the first time to the Earl of Yarborough's son, Lord Worsley.

I can see that boy in my mind's eye now: fourteen years old, tall, slender in build, narrow, handsome, moustachioed features and grey eyes that seemed to glow when they looked at me. I had been narrating the facts behind one of my recent cases of sensation and he was hanging on every word: I realized swiftly that the young man had hero worship in his glance and that . . . well, that's best left for another time. Suffice it to say at this point, that the meeting with Lord Worsley that evening was the first of many, it developed into a close friendship later and was, ultimately, to play a major part in my destruction. . . .

But to return to Marianne.

Pure chance led to our being seated side by side at dinner, although placing me, a *célibataire*, next to a married lady was a little surprising. Normally, it would occur only if her husband was present, of course. It was a sumptuous spread that was laid before us, with a choice of five fine wines during the course of the evening. Viscount Palmerston sat almost opposite me and I was regaled by his political comments on the foreign affairs scene, notably over the Guizot business. But I also noticed that he paid very little attention to the lady on his left: Lady Dacre. Initially, this was a surprise to me. Her placement next to Viscount Palmerston might have been due to a little malice from our hostess. Gossip had it that the Viscount and Lady Dacre had known each other a long time. Since she had been Mistress Brand, in fact, in the days when she had been a lady-in-waiting to the Queen.

The story was, it was the reason why little Vicky disliked Palmerston so much. Her own gaiety and love of dancing had deserted her after she got married to that priggish Prussian Prince Albert: she had taken on board his own view of the undesirability of enjoying oneself too much, other than in the romping privacy of the bedroom, and she was much incensed by the scandal that was visited upon her own palace at Windsor. After dinner on a famous occasion some years earlier, it seems that Lord Palmerston had entered the boudoir of the lady-in-waiting, Mistress Brand, at two in the morning. He had tapped on the door, and when foolishly she had opened to him he had stepped inside, barred the door and commenced to make physical advances to the lady in question. . . .

All under the roof of the Queen at Windsor!

Of course, old Pam had always had a reputation as a Cupid, and was well known to wander the corridors at night when invited to dinner. And quite why Mistress Brand opened the door to him. . . . However, she had screamed, of course, fought off the attentions of the 55-year-old statesman who was just about to get married anyway, and though the scandal was hushed up, the Queen had sternly demanded the dismissal from Government of the corridor-wandering Viscount. The Government of the day resisted it and the incident didn't seem to have damaged his political career much. Or his inclinations towards late-night peregrinations.

However, here they were some years later, Lady Dacre and old Pam, seated side by side and largely ignoring each other. Their studied indifference to each other could have been due to that unfortunate incident at Windsor, but I began to consider a different theory in my head. I was interested in watching them. The coolness they demonstrated to each other seemed odd, and somewhat suspicious to my trained eye. But my attention was distracted for a while, when Marianne broke away from a conversation with her other neighbour, Lord Esher, and lightly touched my arm to attract my attention.

'Mr James, have you heard the news about Lester Grenwood?'

I had not. Since my former friend had fled to the continent after the *Running Rein* affair, to avoid creditors and perhaps a charge of murder I had lost interest in his affairs. He still owed me money, of course, but the days were long since past when I would have hoped that he would honour his debts. I had removed him from my mind, not least because unpleasant memories clung to that whole business: a drowned woman, a disinterred horse, and a man crushed to death on the dockside. . . .

Marianne frowned prettily. She had mastered certain feminine skills since last I had seen her. Now she teased at the lace on her bosom, showed me a little more of the valley between her breasts, turned her large violet eyes on me, held my glance. 'You are aware that I never held Grenwood in high regard. And much disapproved of his friendship with my husband Crosier.'

She had once made her feelings clear to me, before she and Crosier Hilliard had married. I nodded, covertly eyeing the shadowed valley. 'Grenwood, last I heard of him, was in Belgium.'

'Alas,' she sighed theatrically, and unfeelingly, 'he is no longer of this world.'

I grimaced, forgetting the heaving bosom. Grenwood's death meant any tiny hope I had retained of getting my money back had evaporated.

'What happened?'

'It was in Bruges. He fell in the canal. Drowned.'

I was silent for a little while. The irony of his death did not escape me: I still remembered the image of his pregnant mistress being dragged from the Thames by Inspector Redwood. She had committed suicide. Drowned. And now Grenwood had suffered the same fate. I wondered which would have been the dirtier end: the choking black sludge of the Thames, or the clogging muck of a dark canal in Bruges.

'He would have been inebriated, of course,' she said in a muttered tone. 'Why is it that men will so degrade themselves?'

I stared at her. Her eyes met mine. There was a strange glitter in their depths. I had the sudden feeling that she was not speaking of the deceased Lester Grenwood.

We said little more as Lord Esher once again claimed her attention. Across the table, Viscount Palmerston continued to ignore Lady Dacre. She did not seem concerned, though during the course of the dinner there were occasions when her eyes flickered in consternation about the table, and her colour seemed to heighten. There was also the occasional inadvertent twitch of her mouth, a parting of the lips, and from time to time she gave a little jump as though she had been pinched. I noted that these tended to coincide with the occasions when I was unable to see Palmerston's left hand, which from time to time dropped beneath the table while he conversed with the lady on his right.

'So your husband is not able to attend this evening?' I inquired of Marianne, eventually, dragging my attention from the curious events at the other side of the table.

'We were to meet here,' she replied, a little tartly. 'Then I received a note this evening. It seems he is forced to attend to certain military matters in his regiment.'

If I knew Hilliard, they would be taking place in a *bordello* in Panton Street. I did not advise Marianne of my suspicions. She probably held similar suspicions of her own.

The evening proceeded well enough. After dinner we moved into the ballroom, where there was some playing of cards and a little discreet music. Viscount Palmerston sat well apart from Lady Dacre, paying close attention to a much younger woman whose name I have now forgotten. And Lady Dacre seemed not in the slightest interested in conversing with him.

Now, I'd always been of the view that if you wished to maintain secrecy in a liaison, it's a mistake to completely ignore the lady in question even if you think you are being clever in doing so, to avoid suspicion. Particularly if the liaison is the subject of common gossip. I could see that Charles Greville was of the same opinion as me as he cast a worldly eye over the couple. But even Cupids as experienced as old Pam can get things wrong from time to time. The Viscount and the Lady were fooling no one. They would have been wiser to hold occasional conversations: turning their backs on each other only heightened my curiosity, and sharpened my amused suspicions, as well as those of Greville. Particularly after recalling the quickened breathing and the little jumps that had earlier occurred when the Viscount's hand had wandered under the damasked table.

As for myself I took the opportunity to move around the assembly and made sure that I engaged myself in conversation with those whose acquaintance with me was of a narrow nature, but who might be of assistance to me at some time in the future. But rather late in the evening I became aware that there was one person missing from the gathering.

Marianne Hilliard.

I found her on the terrace, beyond the open French windows. She was alone in the cool night air, staring out over the lawns that extended into the darkness. The light from the room fell on her bare shoulders, and the necklace at her throat glittered as I walked towards her.

'Madam, are you well?'

She turned her head slightly, and one hand rose to her throat, as though to caress the necklace, or perhaps to draw attention to the rise of her bosom. The scrap of lace seemed to have disappeared. 'Mr James. I am quite well, thank you. But the heat in that room . . . I thought I would like a little air.'

'Not without a gentleman in attendance,' I replied gallantly.

'I had a desire to be alone.'

'Then I shall withdraw, if you wish.'

She looked directly at me. Her gaze was fixed on mine. There was a certain deliberation in her eyes, which gave me pause. Her slim fingers teased at the necklace. 'No, that would not be my desire, now that you are here.'

I moved towards her, stood at her side, placed one hand on the stone balustrade in front of us. The silence extended; the moon was bright above us, the shadows ahead dark and deep. I felt that there was something in the air, a palpable tension, an uncertainty. And a thought came stealing to me: had Marianne Hilliard stepped out onto the terrace knowing that I would follow her?

'You know my husband well, I believe, Mr James?' she asked quietly after a little while.

The question was unexpected. I was somewhat breathless with anticipation. 'I have known him for some years . . . though not intimately,' I stammered.

'And you knew his boon companion, the unfortunate Lester Grenwood.' There was a bitterness in her tone. After a few moments she added, 'Would it shock you if I were to tell you I do not grieve at Grenwood's demise?'

I was certainly surprised at her expressing the feeling, but I remained silent. The only personal regret I felt over Grenwood's drowning in Bruges was that he had died still owing me money.

'I put it to Grenwood's account that my husband has turned into a dissipated drunkard,' she said with a sudden violence.

The stone of the balustrade was cold under my hand. 'Madam . . . ' I began

She turned to face me. 'My husband will not be at his club this evening, will he, Mr James? The meeting he attends will be of a dissolute nature, a disgraceful, immoral activity which he chooses to undertake rather than join respectable company.'

I had no idea how I should respond, so remained silent.

'For my part,' she said in a strained tone, 'Our marriage began in hope. I was aware of his weaknesses, indeed I was specifically warned about them. But I thought I could draw him away from such companions as Grenwood: I thought I could prevail upon him to give up lascivious pursuits. But as soon as our first child was born I saw less and less of him; a second child did nothing to draw us closer together.' She was silent for a little while. 'My father died two months ago.'

'I'm sorry, Mrs Hilliard. I did not know. . . .'

'He was never a man for Society. But he was a wise and careful man. He had successful investments in banking. And he loved me dearly. The settlements he made . . . Crosier was much disappointed. I know now he married me merely for my . . . prospects. The settlement disappointed him, but I imagine he still had hopes of future inheritances. But my father's will dashed such hopes. My father's death has left me a wealthy woman. And through trustees I can control my own destiny. My husband is unable to interfere, or get his hands on the funds available to me.'

I shuffled, uneasy at the bitterness in her tone. But as she stared at me I felt there was an underlying tension that I found disturbing. And I could not understand why she was speaking of such personal matters in this manner. Then her next words completely sank me.

'I have decided that I shall leave my husband. He shall have an allowance. But I intend to be a free woman.'

My mouth was dry. 'I am sorry to hear of this, Mrs Hilliard. Surely, arrangements can be made for a reconciliation—'

She shook her head. 'It is far too late for that. I am decided. Oh, I'm aware that once I have separated from my husband invitations to evenings such as this will no longer be extended to me. Society will close its doors. It matters not. I intend to take my children and live in Paris. And I shall regard myself as a liberated woman.'

Her eyes held mine. 'A liberated, if occasionally *lonely* woman.'

Now I've already made it clear to you that I was not a man inexperienced in dealings with the tender sex. I had not lacked for relationships with bored wives, thrill-seeking widows or good-time-hunting dollymops. And I was also aware that words between a man and a woman are not necessary in certain situations: it is as though thoughts can be communicated in the ether, intentions laid bare, offers made and accepted without being openly expressed. This was one of those moments. Marianne Hilliard had told me about the collapse of her marriage and her dislike of her drunken, dissolute husband; she had exposed her intention, the manner in which she now intended to conduct her life in future; and buried within this unexpectedly intimate confession was something else, a possibility, an invitation, unexpressed, but there nevertheless.

It was the reason why, some hours later, I was seated in the bedroom assigned to me, with my body on fire, my eyes on the clock, waiting until the house was quiet, the last servants gone to bed, the silence settling on the creaking walls of the old house. She had said nothing direct to me, she had issued no verbal invitation, we had come to no expressed agreement, but I knew in the depths of my soul that she would be expecting me, she would be waiting there silently, in the warm darkness of her room until I came to her.

I tell you, boy, a man experienced in the ways of women knows these things.

So I waited quietly until at two in the dark morning. I picked up my candle and eased open the door of my bedroom, stepped silently into the dark passage beyond.

A single light gleamed on the stairs and cast a faint glow on the high ceiling but the corridor itself was unlit. I had noted earlier that Marianne's room was a little way distant from mine, behind a bend in the corridor, and I moved hesitantly in that direction, shielding the candle with my left hand. I walked on soft feet, slipper-shod, quiet, and the house was silently conspiratorial about me except for the occasional creaks and groans of ancient timbers. I passed a shuttered window and caught a ghostly glimpse of my face, pale, candle-lit, seeming to glow with desire at the thought of the woman who I knew was waiting for me, tense, expectant, willing. . . .

In my careful progress it seemed an age before I reached the corner in the corridor; there I paused, took a deep breath, calmed my excited nerves. It's always thus, isn't it, before you reach the moment of attainment, the satisfaction of an uncertain conquest? I paused, then moved on. The door to Marianne's bedroom was a few yards away. I hesitated again, took a tremulous breath and eased my way around the corner. I walked softly, more quickly now to the door, gathered myself for a moment as my heart hammered, and the blood thundered in my veins, then I raised my hand to tap quietly on the panelled wood.

I never touched the door, for further down the corridor I suddenly caught the gleam of another light.

Biting my lip, I stepped back, quickly snuffed my candle and moved away silently until I regained the cover of the corner I had just rounded. I waited, hardly daring to breathe while I considered what I should do. I still burned for what I was convinced lay waiting for me beyond that bedroom door and I was reluctant to retreat from my prize, seek my own room immediately. Rather, still uncertain, I waited, watching for the approaching dim glow of the shielded candle in the corridor.

He came softly, a thief in the night like me, almost silent on his own slipper-shod feet. He held the candle low in his right hand, extended carefully in front of him as he guided himself with his left hand on the wall beside him. As he approached I could see he was somewhat *deshabillé*, his thinning hair disordered, his baby face shining, his shirt gaping, his pantaloons untrussed. And it was with a sense of shock that I saw him finally pause, then stop uncertainly at Marianne's door. He looked about him, and I cleaved to the dark wall of the corridor. My heart thudded against my ribs as I saw him raise a hand, tap at the panelled door.

There was a long, excruciating pause. He tapped again, lightly still but more urgently and the light of the candle wavered, began to splutter. I thought I detected a rustling sound from inside the bedroom but it might have been my imagination. I caught a glimpse, a gleam of light under the door and then there came the sound of a bolt being carefully withdrawn. There was a brief pause, then the door moved, inched open and the candle in the corridor was raised higher as the man used his free hand to push lightly against the door.

It was then that I recognized him and swore under my breath.

The door slowly opened wide. Marianne stood there like a vision of unbridled desire, her own candle raised to her cheek, the flickering light gleaming on her almost naked shoulders. Her hair was loose, unbraided, and hung about her like a cloud; she wore a shift only, and as I saw her standing there with shadowed, barely covered breasts I knew that I had been right, there on the balcony. Marianne had been expecting me, she had been waiting in the darkness, knowing that I would come to her, feeling what I had been feeling, the churning excitement of a heightening desire. I thought I detected a gleam of tense anticipation in her eyes but as she raised her candle higher I saw the gleam die, to be replaced with a flash of horror as she recognized the man who stood before her.

She gave out a low gasp of distaste. The man in the corridor stood still, transfixed. The candle in his hand shook, sending dancing shadows across the corridor. Unable to contain myself in my own lustful disappointment I stepped forward, eased my way towards the door where Marianne stood thunderstruck, glaring at the surprised man in front of her.

'Madam,' I heard him gasp throatily, 'Lady Dacre—'

Marianne stepped back, still holding the door but her features were frozen with shock. Her glance slipped past the unwelcome intruder and I knew she had caught a glimpse of me in the shadows of the corridor. Then her eyes turned once more to the man who stood helplessly, impotently, in front of her and she raised her head in a gesture of furious pride and closed the door firmly in his face. I heard the bolt slam home with a determined clang.

A burning sensation rose in my throat and I clenched my fists helplessly, frustrated in my desires: I knew Marianne Hilliard would not be opening to another knock that night. I stood just behind the man with the guttering candle and he stepped back, almost colliding with me. He turned and I saw his wide-eyed surprise, as he stared at me, for some moments uncomprehending, failing to recognize me immediately.

Then he bared his ivory false teeth in frustration, disappointment and chagrin. His bald head shook from side to side and he crouched as though his stomach ached in shame. 'The wrong door,' he moaned low in his throat. 'The wrong damned door!'

Making no further acknowledgement of my presence, he turned away and with spluttering candle extended he shuffled away, back down the corridor, mumbling almost incoherently to himself.

I stood watching him till he disappeared. I was trembling with anger and disappointment. I stared at the closed, barred door to Marianne's room. It was an insurmountable barrier to my passion. There was nothing more to be done. I turned away; my stomach was in turmoil as I groped my lonely way back to my bedroom. I found it with some difficulty after clawing ineffectually at several doors along the corridor. I was cold with disappointment, my feverish expectations of a hot encounter dashed, and as I lay at last in my own bed I was unable to sleep, turning, twisting, shifting restlessly against the pillows until the first few slanting gleams of dawn crept in through the shuttered windows, dancing dust motes mocking my restlessness.

I lay sleepless, seeing still in my mind's eye the hunched, despondent form of Viscount Lord Palmerston as he shambled away disconsolately from his expected assignation, and it was only with a sense of personal frustration that I heard over and over in my brain the words he whispered drearily on disappointed lips as he faded slowly into the darkness of the corridor. . . .

'*Je suis foutu! Je suis absolument foutu!*'

PART TWO

1

My younger brother Henry took not to the law but to medicine. He eventually came to specialize in the treatment of female urethral disorders—he was always a man of an exceptionally serious disposition—and I well recall numerous grave late-evening discussions with him regarding my view that sexual connexion was absolutely necessary if one was to prevent atrophy of the testicles. I'm not certain whether these conversations were an attempt on his part to give me some support in the consummation of my evening proclivities or a subtle essay in advising me to slow down, but either way it did nothing to change my ways. After all, wet dreams can be nothing more than a God-given safety valve, and the real thing cannot be surpassed for satisfaction.

Yes, my boy, I've always held that sex is good for a man's health and sexual deprivation is damaging. I've known many women who held the same view, in direct opposition to that fool Acton's comment that the majority of women are not much troubled with sexual feeling of any kind. He had not moved much in high society, I tell you!

Since hearing of my frustration at Lord Yarborough's Friday to Monday, you've expressed some interest in hearing more about that side of my life, and I'm happy to talk about it, on the principle that I can trust you not to mention such matters to your dear mother, of course. Like other young men, my early adventures were in the Strand, naturally enough, because of the slimness of my purse: the ladies of the night who were *habituées* of that area could not be regarded as of the higher class. And there were many street encounters, for the Strand had many corners where the doxies copulated like cattle in the shambles, dark places where low-class whores plied their wares, and relieved themselves afterwards in the gutters . . . the police never interfered, as I recall, unless the encounters occurred in the main thoroughfare.

At the time of my early escapades there were occasional, largely ineffectual attempts by the authorities to clean up the area, and by the time I had progressed to the theatres, where it was possible to pick up the amateurs, the dollymops out for a good time, mingling among the crowd outside, the peelers had begun to force the whores out of Leicester Square and the Strand. It was a pointless exercise, of course, since the ladies simply moved on to the casinos like Evans's and the Holborn and the Argyll Rooms. Pickings were good there, I warrant you: I was able to move on from the £3-whores and make my choice among dancing girls and actresses of note (some of whom, interestingly enough, I later acted for in court). Incidentally, you could always tell the whores at the Argyll Rooms easily enough: they were the ones who left at dawn in cabs.

But the pressure soon moved to these establishments with spoilsports like Macready and Acton making life difficult for them, egging on the magistrates and the police. So it was fortunate for me that I had formed the acquaintance with Cockburn. Along with another couple of lawyers of similar inclination, he'd formed a private Cock and Hen club and eventually I was invited along. He'd taken a lease of discreet premises in St John's Wood and I was invited to join the club where we entertained bored wives in the afternoons, particularly during the Long Vacation. The location was an unexceptional double-fronted villa tucked away in an attractive shady little cul-de-sac. The Club became a sort of *seraglio* for us where four or five young ladies who were uninterested in permanent liaisons (being married to wealthy and usually elderly men more interested in shooting grouse than taking part in erotic adventures) attended for conversations of an intimate character, if you understand what I mean. Port wine, songs around the piano, a rustle of discarded skirts in cool shadowed bedrooms above and post-activity relaxing cigars.

As I recall, I took advantage of Cockburn's Cock and Hen club for perhaps two years, but by 1847, when Cockburn was elected to his seat at Southampton it was no longer convenient for him to enjoy the St John's Wood afternoons. So within a year the villa was regretfully released to other tenants and was no longer available to me, but by then the money from election committee hearings was rolling in and I was of the inclination to find somewhere discreet on my own account. I decided I would look around for a place where I could set up an establishment similar to that which I had enjoyed with Cockburn, where I could entertain whom I pleased . . . and discreetly. I found such a property at Rusper, near Horsham.

The irony of its former history rather pleased me: it had been a retreat for ladies who had taken the veil. The Nunnery, it was called. I rather enjoyed the irony of that, and so did Cockburn. We met there regularly for afternoon assignations with complaisant ladies, drank French and Rhenish wine, smoked excellent Havana cigars and admired the beautiful ladies in their resplendent gowns. Of which we usually divested them in the course of proceedings. And fine fun it was. Thackeray joined us occasionally, as did several members of the Temple. Wilkie Collins came along once. But we kept members of the club few in number, to ensure discretion.

And oddly enough The Nunnery played its part in the next phase of my life, which began when I kept my dinner appointment at the Reform Club with the Attorney General, Sir John Jervis.

As a seaman wandering the oceans of the world, you won't

know the Reform Club in Pall Mall. The magnificent new house was built by Charles Barry in 1841: it opened its membership to Radicals and Liberals; every bedroom had a white marble basin with hot and cold taps and valets always stood by ready to shave and dress you. The famous chef Alexis Soyer ran the kitchen using gas for cooking—quite an innovation then—and there was even a gas flame in a little alcove by the main door where you could light your cigar. Ah, yes, the Reform. . . . I also joined the Garrick, of course, and gambled in Boodles in St James's Street, and I regularly frequented White's as my practice flourished. But the Reform was necessary to pursue my political aspiration: the grand interior entrance, the portraits of eminent former members, the political atmosphere which hung like scented smoke in the air. . . .

Sir John was a gracious host. He did not keep me waiting long in the colonnaded hall of the club, and I was soon ushered into his presence in a small side room occupied only by two elderly gentlemen dozing over editions of *The Morning Post*. He rose to greet me, lean, elegant, affable, gracious of manner, and waved me to a seat at some little distance from the other members. He raised a hand to the attentive waiter, arranged for a brandy and water to be served me, while he contented himself with a glass of Madeira.

'I've been looking back over your career so far,' he mentioned after we had indulged in some polite inanities of the kind which are socially necessary at meetings of gentlemen who are not well known to each other. 'I believe you commenced your practice by concentrating on work in the bankruptcy courts.'

I agreed that this was so.

'And you even chose to write a book on reform of the laws in that sector,' Jervis observed.

I smiled. 'I cannot claim a great success for it. It did not run to a second edition.'

The Attorney General smiled. 'It nevertheless demonstrated two things: one, that you have thought deeply about legal matters of reform, and that you are perhaps thinking of a political career in due course.'

I nodded thoughtfully, fixed a frown of concentration on my features. 'It is why I applied for membership of the Reform Club.'

'Quite so. . . .' A slight, gentle smile touched Sir John's thin lips. 'After you had been blackballed at the Carlton Club.' As I opened my mouth to explain he raised an elegant hand. 'It's quite all right, James. I understand that a young man interested in politics might wish to take his first steps with the party that happens to be forming the Government of the day.' He paused, eyed me reflectively. 'And I understand about the blackballing also. It seems you have made enemies of some powerful people in the Tory party.'

I grimaced. 'One in particular.'

Sir John Jervis nodded. 'Yes. None more powerful. Leader of the Tory Party in the House . . . you refer to Lord George Bentinck. He makes his . . . dislike of you very apparent. From what do you believe this arises?'

I shrugged. 'I suppose it's because I struck at him where he feels himself vulnerable. His love of horse racing.'

Jervis laughed quietly. 'His own father criticized him for years over his attachment to the Turf. And the extent of his gambling, not to mention the low characters he has been involved with at Newmarket and elsewhere. But your verbal blows . . . they arose out of the *Running Rein* affair, I understand.' He eyed me closely. 'Matters there were never satisfactorily resolved, I believe?'

I nodded. I did not feel able to tell him all I knew of the business: the chicanery involved, the body of a woman in the Thames, the beating of a man to death. All that had to remain a secret between me and that unscrupulous villain, Lewis Goodman. To whom I still owed a great deal of tin. I made no reply.

'It's of no consequence,' Jervis remarked after a little while, as he sipped his Madeira and watched me with eyes that seemed to be seeking confirmation of a view. At last, he remarked, 'You are not a close friend of my son.'

'We have met from time to time in Westminster Hall,' I admitted, 'but we are not confidants.'

'Yet you went out of your way to assist him that evening in the Strand.'

I shrugged diffidently. 'It was a matter of circumstance. It's merely chance that brought me into proximity with what happened on that occasion outside the night house. At the tables, I could see that your son was winning a considerable amount of money. And my guess was there was a certain amount of chicanery at the table. He was on a winning run, which would lead him finally to be fleeced. So I thought it wise to step in, advise him he should leave. But then, well, you see, Sir John, it's not been unknown for unscrupulous dealers to reach an arrangement with undesirable characters outside the night house, lurking in the dark. They allow a gull to win a considerable amount and then their confederates outside relieve him of his winnings. The money is then split between the garrotters and the dealer. I cannot be certain that was what occurred that night but your son . . . well, I deemed that he might be vulnerable. It seemed to me to be sensible to make sure that he found himself a cab, when he left. Even without the possible conspiracy I mentioned, the early morning streets can be dangerous.'

I paused: I saw no reason to mention that it had been that villain, Lewis Goodman, who had asked me to take care of young Jervis, nor that the actual physical side of the rescue itself had been largely down to that plug-ugly, Porky Clark.

'In any event, it's beyond dispute that you assisted my son John,' the Attorney General remarked softly, 'and put yourself into danger. That places him, and me in your debt.'

'I would not seek to take advantage of such feelings,' I lied.

The Attorney General raised his glass almost in salute.

'Nevertheless, I feel that I remain in your debt. And I would like to repay you, while, at the same time, suggesting that there is a further service that you might be able to provide me . . . to your benefit, as well as mine.'

'You need only to ask, Sir John.'

'I believe that a little while ago you took the lease of a property at Rusper, near Horsham.'

'That is so. The Nunnery.' I held my breath. I hoped fervently that the Attorney General was not in receipt of rumours concerning the activities that went on in our Cock and Hen Club. And if so, it could hardly be that he desired to join our roistering there . . . or ask that his son be allowed to join us with the ladies.

Sir John Jervis nodded sagely, while I waited, on tenterhooks. He was silent for a little while, twirling his glass between his fingers, as though admiring the colour of the wine it held. At last, he murmured, 'I imagine you are might be aware of the history of the Horsham seat.'

I frowned, and shook my head. 'Only that it is held in the Tory interest.'

'Held? Hardly *held*, in my view. The sitting member, a Mr Hurst, has not been seen by his constituents for some two years. Soon after his election there were rumours of his inability to survive as an MP on account of financial embarrassments. He went abroad and never afterwards took his seat so the borough was effectively disenfranchised. There is a by-election coming up, as a result. The sitting member has been contacted and Mr Hurst has informed the authorities that he has no intention of standing again. So the electors now seek a resident gentleman of independent fortune to represent their interests. A Mr Fitzgerald has recently announced he will stand in the Tory interest.'

I sat very still. 'I had heard something to that effect.'

'The gentleman in question has the strong support of Lord George Bentinck, who will be placing some of his considerable wealth at the disposal of Mr Fitzgerald.'

'Wealth, and the backing of the Leader of the Opposition. A strong combination,' I agreed. There was a stirring in my veins as I watched Sir John twirling his wine glass between his fingers. His expression was thoughtful. 'Mr Fitzgerald,' he murmured, 'has this week issued a notice explaining his position. He has settled in a house at Holbrook, announces he intends to nurse the constituency with ardour, amiability and, no doubt, the results of Lord George's generosity. Naturally, as a Tory Fitzgerald declares himself against Reform.' Sir John's glance rose from his glass and settled almost lazily upon me. 'And naturally our own party will encourage someone of Liberal leanings to oppose him. . . .'

His words died away and yet seemed to hang in the air between us. Beyond the windows I could hear the faint rattle of cabs in the street. The room in which we sat was silent, apart from the occasional rustle of a newspaper being turned by the denizen of a deep leather armchair to our left.

My mouth felt dry. I sipped my brandy and water. My pulse was suddenly hammering as I dwelled on the implications of the silence that now arose between the Attorney General and myself. I had been of assistance to his son. He felt himself indebted to me. He was a senior member of the Government and there was a vacant seat arising where someone of a Liberal persuasion was sought to oppose Lord George Bentinck's lapdog. My thoughts whirled: with Bentinck playing the cards a great deal of money would be spent in this constituency: the eventual winner of the seat would be put to a great deal of expense. I took a deep breath. I was now making a good living at the Bar even if most of my fees seem to drain away before they even reached me, but I had always known that attaining a seat in the Commons would be an expensive business, and at this stage in my career I was not sure I would be able to afford it. But then again, perhaps Sir John would be offering me more than mere opportunity: perhaps he, and other backers, would also be prepared to finance me. The prospect was dizzying.

Sir John Jervis set down his glass. He leaned back in his chair, folded his hands over his waistcoat, twiddled his thumbs reflectively and stared at me with a hawkish expression. 'I have heard good things of you at the Bar, James. You are well on the way to making a great success of your career. You are developing a reputation as a man of courage, conviction and doggedness. The attorneys speak of the quickness of your intellect and sharpness of action. Your name is also spoken of in various social circles. Indeed, Viscount Palmerston himself has been asking me about you: we had a discussion the other evening, when your name came up.'

My breath was tight in my chest. Attorney General Sir John Jervis, and the Secretary for Foreign Affairs, the financial support of the Liberal Party. . . .

'So you have drawn favourable attention to yourself. And as a member of this club, you have shown yourself interested in Reform. So I have a proposal to put to you, which will be, as I have already observed, in both our interests.'

I waited, hardly able to control the excitement in my chest.

'The seat at Horsham. . . .'

I straightened, sat up expectantly, my fingers gripping tightly on the arm of the chair. Sir John was about to speak, when we were suddenly interrupted. Sir John's eyes strayed past me and he smiled warmly, rose to his feet. I looked over my shoulder and saw the tall, slightly stooping figure of Viscount Palmerston coming towards us.

'Ha! Jervis. Dining at the club tonight, hey?' Old Pam's baby face was wreathed in a welcoming smile. The Attorney General rose to his feet and the two men shook hands affably. I rose also.

'You've met Mr James, of course,' Sir John said.

'Indeed, indeed.' Palmerston's almost unwrinkled features were shining below his balding pate and there was a conspiratorial glint in his eyes. 'We met at Lord Yarborough's Friday to Monday, a little while ago.' He raised his bushy eyebrows in query, his glance slipping back to Jervis. 'You'll be talking about Horsham, then?'

The Attorney General smiled and nodded, and I realized that Old Pam had been as fully involved as Sir John in the decision that was being taken that evening. It was confirmed: it was not only the Attorney General who would be supporting me, but also the Secretary for Foreign Affairs.

'So you're on board, hey, James?' Palmerston said affably. His grip was cordial and his eyes held mine. There was a certain mischievous twinkle in them. His next words made me realize why I had his support.

'The party will always welcome young men of ability ... and *discretion.*'

And as I recalled his last words to me, in the dark, two-o'clock-corridor of the home of Lord Yarborough, I knew that my silence on what had occurred that night had been noted, and approved of, and was now being repaid.

Palmerston waved to us both to be seated, but remained standing himself. He put one hand on his hip and wrinkled his nose: there was a hint of sadness in his voice when he next spoke. 'Horsham, ha, yes. I stood there, you know, first election I attempted. It was in 1806 ... long time ago. In those days, you know, there were only seventy-three electors. The borough was in Lady Irving's pocket and she'd previously put up a retired major general, a former Governor General of India, and a West Indian planter fellow. They all stumped up in their turn. Yes, she used to demand a payment of £5,000 each for the two seats in her gift. That year, Lord Edward Fitzherbert and I managed to knock her down: we each put up £1,500 on the understanding that a further £3,500 would be forthcoming if we won, and retained the seats. As it was, we lost, and then, in 1809 the selling of seats was prohibited.'

His eyes lost their faraway look, and he fixed his glance on mine.

'Not that you should misunderstand the situation, James. Damned expensive business, running for Parliament, and Horsham electors have throats of wood. Takes a lot of slaking, that thirst of theirs. So anyone standing for that seat can expect to dig deep into his pockets. Bentinck—'

'Has declared for Fitzgerald and will back him financially,' Sir John asserted.

Palmerston was silent for a few moments, nodding thoughtfully. Then he smiled, held Jervis's glance conspiratorially, and nodded. 'Well, we'll have to see what can be done about things on our side,' he murmured.

He took a deep breath, straightened and nodded affably to us both. 'I'll leave you to it, then. Lady Palmerston is expecting me at Stanhope Street, and I'm already late. But that's the life of a politician, hey?'

He was well known for driving himself hard in office: his clerks hated him for the manner in which he drove them too. After all, as young men of good connections they had entered the Civil Service in expectation of sinecures, but life was not like that under Old Pam.

The Attorney General and I sat down again after he had left us. I was now almost quivering with excitement. I would have the support of two senior members of the party, and the weight of the Whigs behind me. I had every confidence: it would be impossible for me to lose, even with Bentinck's malign influence directed against me.

Next moment, my house of cards fell in.

'Ah, where were we?' Sir John asked blandly. 'Ah, yes, the seat at Horsham.' He looked at me, and smiled. 'We have decided upon a person to oppose Mr Fitzgerald.' His eyes held mine steadily. There was a short, pregnant pause. 'I intend that my son John should put himself forward at Horsham as a candidate in the Liberal interest.'

I was unable to prevent the gasp of crushing disappointment

which escaped from me. The Attorney General hardly seemed to notice it. His gaze was now fixed on the ceiling, as though he was considering matters of import. 'There will be many who will say John is too young, of course, and inexperienced . . . and there is some truth in that, as we have seen from his behaviour in that night house. So he will need strong support, a steadying hand, a man who can guide him through stormy waters, avoid the dangerous rocks that might sink his candidature. At the night house you recognized the dangers facing him and your quick thinking rescued him there from the consequences of his folly. I have discussed the matter at length with Lord Palmerston and we are both agreed. I now ask in confidence if you would be prepared to support my son once more, this time in the political arena. For the good of the Liberal Party, and of my family.'

My mouth was dry with the sand of my disappointment. I hesitated, mumbling, 'I'm not sure what—'

'I would like you to become John's political agent for the Horsham by-election.'

I stared blankly at the Attorney General. The proposal, after the sabre-cut of disappointment I had suffered, came out of the blue. And for a few moments all I could think of was the effect such a situation would have upon my avowed enemy, Lord George Bentinck.

Sir John observed me serenely. 'You have been active on the election committees often enough to know what is required of a good Parliamentary Agent, not merely to persuade the voters but also to steer the candidate well away from the rocks of folly. You have seen many successful candidates unseated on appeal; indeed, you have made your own contribution in that matter. So your experience will be invaluable to young John. We would provide you with the necessary supporting finance, of course. We would use your residence at Rusper as campaign headquarters, for an appropriate fee, naturally. You would take upon yourself the duties incumbent on an agent, undertake the masterminding of the campaign, and in so doing you would be in receipt of my considerable gratitude once more. My gratitude, and that of the Party.'

But not the seat itself. I fought down the feeling of disappointment, almost unable to speak. But, slowly, I rallied, keeping my head down so he could not see what my eyes might betray. Not a seat in Parliament . . . but a parliamentary agent for the son of the Attorney General. There would still be something I could obtain out of this opportunity. I raised my head.

In the pause that grew about us, Sir John Jervis eyed me carefully as though I was a witness before him in court. After a little while, he said, 'That gratitude can thereafter be shown in several ways, of course. There is first the matter of Treasury briefs. Your name has already been noted as that of a rising talent in the courts, and the Treasury solicitors are already aware of your abilities. It requires only a word from certain quarters to ensure that such briefs in future become more numerous, as far as you are concerned.'

I ran my tongue over dry lips, but was still unable to speak. A mixture of disappointment and elation still swept over me and my thoughts were confused.

'And then there is the matter of legal and political advancement,' the Attorney General continued. 'Once my son is safely installed at Horsham we will have opportunity to look at your own personal interests in such matters. There's first the matter of extending your experience: I think there's the possibility of considering you for a Recordership in due course . . .' He paused. 'In fact, the Recordership of Brighton will become vacant in a little while.'

My earlier disappointment was rapidly fading as his words, and their implications, sank into my brain. I was still a junior barrister and had not taken silk, but if I was to be considered for a Recordership that additional honour, Queen's Counsel, would have first to be conferred upon me. And as a Recorder I would have taken the first step towards a seat as one of Her Majesty's judges. The prospect was dazzling: Queen's Counsel, a Recordership and then. . . .

'And then, a General Election cannot be too far away. Seats will become available, important metropolitan seats, even. Lord Palmerston and I will be able, and willing, to place our influence behind you, and I suspect there are others in the party who would not be averse to giving you additional support.'

Such as Alexander Cockburn, I surmised. As a sitting Member for Southampton, a rising political star and a member of our Cock and Hen Club, he would put in a good word for me, I was certain. And, it was rumoured, he was already being touted for a seat on the bench in the near future. If he was so elevated, his seat at Southampton would fall vacant. It could fall to me. Or one of the metropolitan seats, as Sir John had suggested. There were so many possibilities. . . . I took a deep breath, deciding to seize chances wherever they might arise. In spite of my disappointment over the candidature for Horsham, the prospects suddenly dangled before me were heart-stopping and the support of the Attorney General and the Foreign Secretary were powerful incentives to agree to the proposition.

I held up my head, jutted out my pugilist chin confidently. 'I shall be honoured and delighted to take on the task you offer me,' I said firmly. 'Your son is a fine young man, and I am certain he will prove to be an ornament of the party when he is once in Parliament. As his agent, I will do the utmost in my power to bring about his success.'

There was a short silence, then Sir John Jervis smiled broadly. He rose, extended his hand and took mine in a firm handclasp. 'Then that's settled, James. You must come around to a private meeting at my house, to discuss matters with my son John and certain of our friends. I am certain he, and they, will be as pleased as I that you accede to this request. And now, perhaps we should go in to dinner.'

To be honest, I have no great recollection of our conversation over dinner, though oddly enough the repast itself has remained in my memory: turtle soup, turbot, three meat dishes, lobster *vol au vent*. I remember also the raspberry cream and orange water ices. Otherwise, the occasion passed as a blur and I was barely able to hold up my end of the conversation. I thought Sir John was aware of my confusion, and took no offence at my apparent woolly-mindedness. But the fact was his comments had opened up to me glittering professional vistas. A seat in the House of Commons would not only further and promote my career but it would enable me to deal with my creditors in a more effective manner: they would not be able to dun me as a sitting Member of Parliament. More, with the support of the Government a commission from the Crown as Queen's Counsel would be swift, and if Sir John kept his word and arranged for my appointment as Recorder I was confident that my ability would soon lead to a seat on the bench, where I would join my friend Alexander Cockburn. I could see the future flashing before my inner eye: Queen's Counsel, a Recordership, then in due course a judicial appointment, or, once I had attained a seat in the House, the post of Solicitor General in a future administration, then Attorney General and finally even Lord Chief Justice, or Lord Chancellor!

It was all there before me, there for the taking.

The curious thing that struck me later was that in a way this had all come about as a result of the intervention of that villain, Lewis Goodman ... whom, one day in the future, *Deo volente*, I might have the opportunity of sending to a damp, noisome cell where he would spend the rest of his days in a place he deserved so richly.

2

Listen. I don't wish you to be misled about what happened there-after at Horsham. Much was later written about it, but nothing occurred during that by-election that had not happened before, in other constituencies. Though perhaps not to the same degree, I admit. I had seen more than enough evidence of the results of election fever, on the election committees in which I had gained a reputation, where took place the unseating of successful candidates on the ground of bribery and corruption of the voters. But that was the way things were ordered in those days. And it was a minion of Lord George Bentinck, inevitably, who began the campaign later, when all the Horsham shouting was over, a campaign of denigra-tion, the use of half-truths and downright lies, even a resort to the courts, in his fury that I had been so successful. He made a bad enemy, his Lordship. And there were always hangers-on, political nonentities prepared to do his bidding.

As to the manner in which I ordered things during the campaign, well, Bentinck's fury was made so much the greater because I showed myself to be a better organizer than his men, more efficient in my arrangements and a more ruthless opponent than he could have imagined. A knowledge of the rough and tumble world of the prize ring and the racecourse was useful; an ability to indulge in the dirty tricks of the Old Bailey courtroom was essential. And the wit and sagacity to act before your opponent was the clinching ability.

I was early out of the blocks in the three weeks before the by-election. Mr W. R. S. Fitzgerald, the Tory candidate with the foxy, side-whiskered features and aggrieved air, issued a nebulous kind of address to the constituents where he claimed to be a Whig to the Whigs, a Tory to the Tories and a Protectionist to the Protectionists but I immediately persuaded Sir John Jervis himself to come down to Horsham to speak in support of his son. I wrote the speech he delivered. It was well received. Sir John had been MP for the city of Chester since 1832 and was an old electioneering campaigner and it proved to be a shrewd move on my part. The Attorney General presented himself with confidence and determination, announced the candidature of his son and gave out the words I had written: 'I have never yet lost an election and I intend not to lose this one!'

It was a slogan that appealed to the cheering crowd before they repaired to the Anchor Inn for the usual refreshments.

The next thing to do was to appoint a small committee on whom I could rely. Sir Alexander Cockburn was the first to figure on my list: I also brought on board a local solicitor with an extensive range of social contacts, a Mr Medwin, who had a spreading belly and an air of sagacity, which he backed with a sharp, calculating mind. It was on his recommendation that I added to the group a local man, Mr Lintott, who was in close touch with other landowners of consequence as the largest and richest tradesman in the town, flattered to be brought in to work with such elevated company. But we also needed an enforcer. It was for that reason I turned to my old acquaintance, Ben Gully.

He came down for a private conference with me at the Black Horse Hotel. He had dressed for the occasion, out of town. He wore a dark, well-cut greatcoat and dark corduroy breeches, while his black kid gloves demonstrated he was a man of business. He could not disguise the rearranged features, of course, the result of various violent encounters in dark corners of the city, but there were many gentlemen of quality who sported broken noses and fractured jaws: after all, it was a matter of honour in those days that young gentlemen should familiarize themselves with the pugilistic arts. In Ben's case, however, his battering had not taken place under the rules of the Marquis of Queensbury.

He eyed me carefully, one eye wandering as usual as he scanned the room, while I explained the position.

'It's like this, Ben. The organization of the campaign will be masterminded by me, and I have formed a small committee that will be able to determine on tactics and indeed, counteract the actions of our opponents. But inevitably there will come occasions when plans can go awry, when tactics fail, and when—to put it plainly—a certain degree of action will be demanded. And for that, we shall need a determined fellow who will be able to act swiftly and decisively.'

Ben Gully took a swallow of his porter and grunted doubtfully. 'Thing is, Mr James, politics ain't really my field.'

'The back streets of any town or city are not much different from others. Cudgels come out, drunkards get waylaid, pockets get picked and . . . electors can get *persuaded*. I need someone who can keep an eye on that sort of thing, advise me, and if necessary take action himself, and quickly.'

'He'll need something about him, other than his fists,' Gully said thoughtfully. 'If he's going to mingle successfully with gentlemen.'

'A well-known member of the swell mob won't do, Ben.'

'I see that, Mr James. On the other hand . . . you ever have dealings with a Captain Thomas?'

I grimaced, shook my head.

Gully grunted. 'I transacted a certain business lately, which brought me into contact with Captain William Lanham Thomas, late of the Indian Army.' His glance rose, fixed upon mine. 'On half-pay now. Possibly left India under a cloud. Rumour speaks of mess funds not properly accounted for.'

So probably needing money. I frowned. A gentleman, an ex-officer, not well known in London society. . . . 'A hard man?'

'I seen some evidence of it,' Ben Gully remarked almost casually.

'You can recommend him?'

I had a deal of confidence in Ben Gully. No one knew the London scene as he did. No one knew the back alleys and the rookeries of St Giles, the tricks of the magsmen and the sharps, the bullies and the pimps. But he also knew those who lived on the edges of the underworld, gentlemen who had fallen on hard times, men of quality who now dealt in doubtful activities to make a living; others who sought to climb the social ladder from the villas in St John's Wood that they had acquired with fortunes won at the edge of legality. I trusted Ben's judgment because it was based on solid knowledge.

After a short silence, Ben murmured, 'I think he would serve your purpose, Mr James.'

I met Captain William Lanham Thomas on the Friday of that same week.

I got to know him quite well in the weeks that followed our agreement to work together in support of young John Jervis's campaign. The gallant captain had indeed returned from India some months previously and was still settling into a gentlemanly routine. The captain was not experienced in election campaigns, of course, but I soon learned that he was shrewd, decisive and showed on occasion a fierce determination to get what he wanted. Nor was he averse to the odd scuffle. He was some six feet in height, of a lean muscular stature, had fine whiskers that denoted the gentleman but he knew his common man, and he had an air of cold-eyed efficiency that proved more than useful in the campaign.

That day of our first acquaintance, I had the feeling that he was weighing me up as much as I was him.

'So Mr Jervis has considerable political backing,' he observed coolly.

'Certainly.'

'And that will mean access to sources of considerable funds.'

'The campaign will be more than adequately funded,' I admitted.

'So there will be no problem of payment. You will note, Mr James, I am a practical man.'

If not a complete gentleman. But I knew what it was like to be dunned by creditors. We quickly agreed upon matters of recompense for the captain's involvement.

'And what exactly will be my duties?' he inquired, his glacial blue eyes fixed carelessly upon mine.

'You will be a member of the campaign committee but will not advise on tactical matters. Rather, you will be our ear to the ground, the supplier of information regarding the activities of the other side, our adviser on methods to prevent the accomplishment of Mr Fitzgerald's designs, whatever they might be, and the man who will see to it that what is necessary to be done, will be done.'

He smiled coldly, and stroked his luxurious moustache gently with a loving forefinger. 'I gain the impression, sir, that this work would not greatly interfere with my predilection towards the frequenting of racecourses, public houses and gambling dens, convivial gatherings of *ouvriérs* in public houses and the occasional bout of fisticuffs.' As he spoke he twirled in his hand the cane he carried: the knob was of solid brass, and I suspected it was a sword cane. His meaning was quite clear to me.

'You are a man after my own heart, Captain Thomas.'

Ben Gully had chosen and recommended well.

And indeed, Captain Thomas soon proved himself to be an efficient tool in our hands, in most cases acting discreetly so no blame could attach, and after the Horsham campaign I came across him from time to time, though I never had occasion to employ him further. I had the honour of representing him in court on a few occasions, in affairs both of the heart and honour, in which a degree of violence on his part had proved inevitable, and you could say we had become close acquaintances at a certain level. I knew he would be a useful addition to the team should the expected difficulties arise during the campaign. I gave him no hand in the preparation of the candidate's election address for that was not his *forte*, but I knew full well his strong arm would come in useful. But I'll come to that later.

Sir John Jervis had assured me that money was not a problem, so once he had called in favours from a few local friends we began our first canvass of the local electorate. This necessitated approaching every public house and beer shop in the parish, flying flags and Blue favours and agreeing that the publicans should keep their cellars open to all: if a voter required a drink it should be supplied and the bill sent on to me.

We began with the attractively meaningless slogan *Independence for the Borough* and slandered Fitzgerald politically and personally with strong drink. I set up our first champagne dinner at the Anchor Hotel, served wine, brandy, punch and laid down the basis for numerous headaches next morning. At the Black Horse I called an Amalgamation Dinner to celebrate the fact that we had already managed to bring over to our side a number of Pink electors who had previously supported Fitzgerald. The dinner— which included salmon, duck, chicken, ham and tongue—was held with Mr Medwin in the chair: there was an elegant spread, numerous healths were drunk to, toasts were given and plans were laid for attracting as many voters as possible to the Jervis and Liberal cause. My account book showed payment for one hundred and twenty-four bottles of wine, thirty-eight bowls of punch and a considerable quantity of ale and stout as I laid down the basis for what a sour Lord George Bentinck was already castigating as 'sinister and daring activities'.

While my committee worked from The Nunnery at Rusper, we fixed our campaign headquarters, for obvious reasons in view of the anticipated thirst of the voters, at the Crown Hotel. I then established agents, sub-agents and friends at as many beer shops as we were able in the parish: the Crown, the Star, the Shelley Arms, the Horse and Groom, the White Horse and the Red Lion among others and all were thrown open to voters, the cellars were filled to capacity and the Brewers and Spirit Merchants were warned that during the ensuing weeks there would be an uncommon run on their commodities. They duly brought in new stock.

Our Tory opponent, Fitzgerald, was not idle, of course, in that respect: the Pinks claimed the Black Horse, the Swan, the Green Dragon and the Dog and Bacon among other hostelries, so never let it be said, as Bentinck's lapdog politicians later averred, that the treating and drunkenness in the Horsham election was all one-sided. During the run-up to the election it soon became established that a voter of either persuasion or none could go to any public house and obtain any kind of refreshment he desired without offering payment, for the landlords knew where they would obtain financial satisfaction. It was inevitable, of course, that lovers of small beer now discovered more aristocratic beverages; friends were encouraged to join in parties of five or more and it quickly became apparent to me that lemonade-and-brandy was becoming the most popular beverage, the new fashionable drink in Horsham. So it was soon a common sight during those weeks to see these lemonade-and-brandy politicians staggering along the pavements en route to yet another public house of refreshment. Wives brought out jugs and visited the houses, or sent their children to collect refreshment in the name of our candidate. Fitzgerald soon cottoned on to the practice and began to urge a similar pattern on his prospective supporters.

A number of side bets were laid down at the time, which Captain Thomas closely monitored by personally attending the taverns and hostelries and when the swell of opinion was reported to me I knew we had to canvass more widely. As a consequence I instituted a series of public meetings. The first was at the Crown; the third, a really big 'do', was at the Anchor Hotel.

We arrived in a four-horse coach: pale-featured young John Jervis, gallantly moustached Captain Thomas and the portly Mr Medwin, together with 'Bulldog' Cockburn and 'Big-Headed' Jimmy as we two lawyers were now nicknamed by frequenters of the taverns. The main room of the Anchor was packed with all conditions of men. I had previously ordered one hundred bowls of punch and John Jervis was proposed, seconded, adopted, toasted and all were thereafter given wine, brandy, punch and cigars, to everyone's satisfaction. Songs were roared out and speeches given and although formalities were concluded by 10 p.m., the carousing continued well into the early hours of the morning.

The locals soon roared out a ditty, sung to the tune of *Buffalo Girls*. I remember it well:

Horsham Boys won't you come out tonight
Come out tonight, come out tonight,
Horsham boys won't you come out tonight
For a drunk with Jervis and James.

Of course, I should have foreseen that when other landlords noted the success of the Anchor 'do' they would clamour for similar opportunities to be granted them and we were forced to continue, as Fitzgerald followed in our train. There were big 'dos' at the chief Inns and Hotels, and small 'dos' in the beer shops. Handsome suppers, drinks and cigars interspersed with speeches were the order of the day. But when Fitzgerald saw that we were lopping off a number of his followers, whatever sense of ethics he held deserted him and his supporters.

And that's when it all began. I got blamed for it later, of course, but I swear it was Fitzgerald who started the real skulduggery. With Bentinck backing him to the hilt. On the other hand, I suppose I have to admit I was better at it than his agent was, and Captain Thomas soon proved his mettle.

The crunch came at a 'do' at the Shelley Arms. I was determined to outdo whatever Fitzgerald had been able to offer. On that one evening our liquor consumption was extraordinary, not least because railway navigators working on the Three Bridges to Horsham line joined us in some numbers; I was upstairs at supper with young John Jervis—who was roaring drunk—Mr Medwin, Cockburn and several voters of consequence while the rooms below were crowded with electors and their hangers-on, many outside struggling to gain entrance, some fighting over ladders to get in at upstairs windows. It was a scene of roistering, good-natured pandemonium and the Nuthurst Band of about nine players was performing joyously on the green outside as brandy was served to all in wine glasses and tumblers. I had just personally performed the song *The Old English Gentleman* and was standing on a table.

'May I propose the health of Mrs Whiting and the ladies of Horsham!' I roared.

Mrs Whiting was actually a chimneysweep's wife who kept the Travellers Rest beer shop and I'd just caught sight of her filling a kettle with punch to take home. Others were collecting up baskets of pickled salmon, duck, chicken, ham, tongue. Grog was being ladled into tea cups from pails, and there were some inevitable disagreements downstairs, settled by some of Captain Thomas's 'convincers' armed with the legs of smashed chairs. It was all part of the game. As I waved my glass from the vantage point of the table and cheers resounded and further toasts were called for, Cockburn, who was well in his cups at the time, tapped at my leg.

'Get down from there! Get down!' he roared.

'What's the matter?'

'Captain Thomas,' he shouted against the roar of the drunken revellers. 'He's downstairs. He wants to talk to you. Matter of urgency.'

And urgent it certainly proved to be.

I finished my glass of champagne and made my way down the stairs. I was directed to a small snug behind the taproom. Captain Thomas was waiting for me there. His necktie was astray, and there was a red mark below his left eye. I closed the door behind me: he and I were alone together.

'There's been trouble?' I asked gesturing towards his eye.

'Nothing I couldn't handle, Mr James. Constable Green. It seems he was concerned about the noise and the goings-on upstairs and came in to make inquiry.'

'I suppose that's his job.'

'I think he's been got at by the Pinks,' Captain Thomas observed. 'And we had words. High words.'

'What happened?'

'He wanted to go upstairs. I told him to sling his hook. He decided to make an issue of it. I presented him with some . . . ah . . . unmentionable compliments and advised him to leave. It's then he swung his stick at me.' He fingered the red swelling below his eye: there was a malicious glint in the glance he gave me. 'I escorted him from the premises. Firmly. Last I saw he was sitting in the mud in the Market Square.'

Not very wise, I thought, but what's done is done. 'I leave such matters to you, Captain. Is that why you called me down here?'

The gallant officer shook his head. 'No. The fact is, there's things you need to be apprised of. Mr Fitzgerald is raising the stakes.'

'In what way?'

'I think it best you listen to my informant.'

He turned aside, opened the door and stepped outside into the narrow passage beyond. I heard a murmured conversation and a short while afterwards Captain Thomas returned. With him was a big, red-faced man who was holding his billycock hat in his hands. But there was nothing subservient about him: shifty, yes, but he had determined eyes and, I guessed, a hard, unscrupulous heart.

'Mr James, may I present Charlie Feist.'

We did not shake hands. I stared at the newcomer. While I had no recollection of having previously met him, the name had a familiar ring. After a moment alarm bells began to chime in my head: this man had a reputation. We stood there in silence in the dimly lit room while I dredged for recollections, stories of previous events, earlier elections. . . .

'Charles Feist,' I murmured. 'A former shoemaker, I believe.'

'Them days is behind me, Mr James.' His voice was hoarse and deep.

'Ah, yes,' I replied as stories came flooding back into my head. 'I believe you're now known as *Lawyer* Feist, having attached yourself to a legal office after working as a bum-bailiff.'

'I knows a bit of law,' Feist admitted

And I knew about Charlie Feist. At every contested election of recent years in Horsham he had played an active and prominent part—though not always on the same side. He cut his coat according to the money he could make from that garment: he weighed up and compared the prospective benefits to be obtained from each party before declaring his allegiance. He claimed an intimate knowledge of the borough and to be able to bear influence on a considerable number of voters, come polling day. I also knew that in this particular election he had already been active in our opponent's behalf.

'I also knows, the way things is running, that there's only about six votes in it, at present,' he added in a low growl.

You must appreciate that in those days before voting reform the eligible voters in Horsham numbered only some four hundred, and my own estimate at that point in time agreed with that of Charlie Feist. I shrugged. 'So why is it you want to see me?'

Charlie Feist hesitated, glanced at Captain Thomas, and then boldly announced, 'I received £40 cash from Mr Nelthorpe, for my support of Mr Fitzgerald and the Pinks.'

'I had heard you were in that camp,' I murmured disdainfully.

'Thing is, I got a grudge against Nelthorpe: he defrauded me out of possession of a new cart.'

I doubted that, but remained silent.

'And I don't approve of what's going down.'

I glanced at Captain Thomas; his cold eyes held a hint of the cynicism he clearly felt. I grimaced. 'So. . . ?'

'I considers I might be able to be of some assistance to Mr Jervis in his bid.'

It was there, unsaid, but clear enough to me. Feist had taken Nelthorpe's gold, but had concluded that the Attorney General in his more eminent position would in the long run be more able to provide greater prospective benefits to Charlie Feist. He confirmed my suspicion when he went on, 'I'm well in with the other side. But I don't like what they're planning. And it occurs to me that it might be to Mr Jervis's advantage if I was to, well, sort of act as your eyes and ears in the Fitzgerald camp.'

A spy.

I weighed it up in my mind. There would be a price to pay, although money was no problem on our side. I would not be able to get personally involved, of course, but as I held Captain Thomas's glance I knew he could clearly see that I approved of this meeting with the slimy ex-shoemaker. But the question was, to what extent could we trust the nimble-footed Lawyer Feist?

Captain Thomas was watching me and was aware of my doubts. He nodded. He put a hand on Feist's shoulder. 'I would like a word with Mr James. If you would care to wait in the taproom, I'll see you there in a few minutes.'

'The stable yard,' Feist suggested. 'Wouldn't want to be seen at this Jervis 'do', Cap'n.' He eyed me briefly, seemed to be about to say something, thought better of it, and then left the room.

Captain Thomas sighed, twirled a finger in his gallant moustaches. 'Scum, but perhaps a useful ally. We can never trust him of course, but he could provide us with useful information. At a price.'

'Are you certain of that?'

Captain Thomas bared his teeth in a wolfish grimace. 'He's come with information for free. As a token. It's why I needed to see you, Mr James. I could have dealt with Feist myself, otherwise, but I need a decision from you.'

'How do you mean?'

'This upping of the stakes by the Fitzgerald camp. Feist tells me they've decided to take other steps than give out drink and hard cash: they've taken on some outside assistance.'

'Such as?'

'They're bringing in out-of-town thugs. In the next few weeks, coming up to the hustings, they're going to place men at every road leading out of Horsham and search any trap suspected of conveying voters out of the town. They're going to attack us where we're weak: they're going to steal voters, threaten them, whisk them away to hotels in London, lock them up if necessary.'

'What sort of numbers are we talking about here?' I asked.

'Feist reckons they're planning about twenty on duty each night, some on horseback, some even disguised as women in distress so as to stop a conveyance.' He paused. 'Feist tells me they've already got hold of the landlord of the Dog & Bacon, and there's five voters been *persuaded* to stay at Springfield Park until polling day's past. The gamekeeper at Denne Park, who promised his vote to us, he's also been captured. The pressure is on, Mr James. We need to respond, if Feist is correct in the numbers game.'

'He's correct,' I replied briskly. 'What do you recommend?'

'You leave it to me. We'll take up Feist's offer, to obtain regular intelligence. I'll draft in some acquaintances, and anyone you can recommend. With your experience in the Old Bailey and your knowledge of Newmarket I'm sure you'll be familiar with some useful characters who might be able to serve with us.'

I gave him a sharp look, but he was right. We needed more muscle. I considered briefly. I nodded. 'It's in your hands. I'll need a receipt for what we pay Feist but make it . . . unobjectionable. As for names . . . there's a man called Ned Evans. And there's Sam Martin and Porky Clark. The sight of those three swaggering around Market Street in Horsham will make up a few minds, I don't doubt.'

Captain Thomas nodded, his eyes glittering. 'And meanwhile, there's the urgent matter of Job Pickett.'

The name was familiar. I frowned. 'The cowman at Holbrook? The one who refused to support Fitzgerald and was turned out of his job by the bailiff? We've been looking after him—'

'Not well enough. He's disappeared. But Feist knows where he is, and if we take on Charlie Feist, we can do what's needed for our supporter, Job Pickett.' He smiled grimly. 'It will be a little operation you yourself might wish to take part in, Mr James. You're well known to be a sporting man.'

3

And that's really how it all moved into a new stage of proceedings.

It began with Job Pickett, and as Captain guessed I was interested in personally going on the raid, partly out of sheer curiosity; partly to discover just how reliable our new recruit Charlie Feist could be. It turned out his information was sound.

There were nine in our party, well-armed with cudgels and knob sticks, and I suspected at least two of the group, apart from Captain Thomas, were carrying concealed firearms. We travelled by gig to Holbrook, the estate where Fitzgerald had established his home and political headquarters, by way of Southolme where we picked up the cowman's wife. She was a sturdy broad-bosomed woman and a determined one and as we rattled onwards to Holbrook under the pale light of the evening moon she explained what had occurred to her husband.

'Mr Fitzgerald, he threatened to turn Job out of his work as cowman at Holbrook if he voted for Mr Jervis, but when Job was adamant for the Blues he threatened to turn us out of the cottage. But Sunday morning a message came calling him to Holbrook where Mr Fitzgerald would make him a new offer. When he got there I'm told by the butler that he was treated well, plenty of food and drink, promised a new rig-out for hisself and me and a fortnight's holiday, but my Job is a stickler, you know, and when he refused to change his mind, well, they locked him up in the cellar!'

Captain Thomas leaned towards me in the swaying, lurching trap. 'That's when she contacted me. She'd got worried when he hadn't returned on Sunday evening, went up to the house and was refused entrance. It seems, Mr James, it would not be to our advantage if we were to leave this matter stand. We need to show our determination. We have no choice but to make a frontal attack.'

Now I have to admit, my boy, that this seemed to me to be taking things too far but the Captain's blood was up and so I did not demur as we rattled along the stony lanes until we were about a half-mile from the big house. As our master strategist and an Army man, Captain Thomas ordered our dispositions: five men to take various positions around the house in the darkness; the other four to march straight up to the front entrance.

With some trepidation, but without comment, I accompanied the storming party.

To my surprise, the gallant captain made no attempt to seek permission to enter: we marched up to the imposing doors and when Captain Thomas pushed out his hand, the unlocked door gave way, so we found ourselves unopposed in the echoing hallway of Holbrook House. The astonished footman, one John Fry, was the first to come rushing out from the parlour where he had been attending his master. When Captain Thomas demanded to know where Job Pickett was being held he was quickly joined by a distraught butler, named, I recall, Robert Dawes. Strange how I remember these names after all these years . . . but then, they both gave evidence at the subsequent legal proceedings.

There we were in the hallway, a group of belligerent, grimacing, cudgel-armed villains headed by Captain Thomas, with me lingering in a strategic position a little way behind. Dawes dashed into the parlour and slammed the door. We waited a short while, the captain declaiming in a high, somewhat inebriated tone, that his blood was up and he would see justice done by the release of an Englishman who was unjustly incarcerated. I had vague thoughts of *Habeas Corpus* and also *Trespass* writs floating around in my head, well aware that they would hardly serve in this situation, when finally the parlour door opened and a pale-faced, shaken Fitzgerald appeared before us, in smoking jacket and slippers. Our Tory candidate had a fire poker in his trembling hand.

'You have intruded upon my *home,* sir!' he challenged, somewhat tremulously.

'To come to the aid of an imprisoned friend,' Captain Thomas roared, waving his cudgel and flicking at his coat tails, allowing the pistol thrust into his belt to appear as though by chance.

'I have no idea what you are talking about,' Fitzgerald replied lamely, his voice shaking in turn with his hands.

'By God!' railed the Captain, waving his cudgel in an arc above his head, 'you lie in your teeth and you'll release Job Pickett this instant or I'll see your head bloodied and your—'

'*Captain!*' I said and stepped forward, placing a restraining hand on his arm. Things were going forward too hastily. I turned to our political opponent. 'We have Mrs Pickett with us. She waits outside in the garden. She has informed us that her husband is detained here . . . for political purposes. Now it may well be that she is mistaken, that he is perhaps drunk, or unwell, and perhaps this is all a mistake. . . .'

I allowed my voice to die away. Captain Thomas was glaring at me, clearly furious at the opportunity lost if I were to continue to mollify the man into whose house we had stormed. Silence fell, and Fitzgerald stood there, shuddering, whey-faced, and somewhere in the house a window banged. Fitzgerald heard it and swallowed hard. He took a deep breath and grimaced. 'Mr James . . . I must ask you to lead these friends of yours from this house. This is a blackguardedly outrage and—'

'We seek only the release of Job Pickett,' I remonstrated.

'The man is not here,' Fitzgerald asserted through grinding teeth.

I waited. Then, slowly, gently, I said, 'Mr Fitzgerald, if you can give me your word as a gentleman, that Job Pickett is not to be found on the premises, we will immediately withdraw.'

Captain Thomas snorted in derision, but Fitzgerald swallowed hard, looked me in the eye and after a brief silence, in a low, defeated voice he said, 'I give you my word as a gentleman, Mr James. Job Pickett is not on the premises.'

We both knew what he meant, but there was a gusty sigh of disappointment from my companions. The thugs that Captain Thomas had brought with him were clearly chagrined that the game was to be given up so easily. The Captain himself was far from pleased. But I knew we were on shaky ground legally, and it was best to withdraw: where a man's home was concerned, it was unwise to use military tactics to obtain entrance. And I had heard the window bang. I led the way out through the open front door. It was slammed shut behind us by butler Dawes.

'So where the hell does that get us, Mr James?' Captain Thomas demanded fiercely. 'We have retreated in ignominy!'

As though in answer, a loud whistle came to us from the darkness of the shrubbery on the south side of the house. Then I made out the tone of a shrill, scolding woman. It seemed that Mrs Pickett was not too pleased to have her husband returned after all, at least, not in the state of staggering inebriation in which she had found him, unceremoniously shoved out of the ground floor window when our determination in the hallway had been demonstrated.

'We had no choice. Mr Fitzgerald gave us his word,' I said to Captain Thomas. 'At least, once he knew the servants had thrown Pickett into the shrubbery.'

So we loaded our drunken supporter into one of the traps, along with his wife, and we conducted the two heroes first to the Star and then to the Crown where after a suitably triumphant carousal we ended up with a supper of pickled salmon and broke up the party only at four in the morning.

And so the tone was set.

We matched Job Pickett's incarceration by locking up the landlord of the Dog and Bacon for a fortnight. Five other voters were confined in similar fashion at Springfield Park until polling day, well provided with food and drink, of course. We kept George Elphick and Robert Parsons in London for two weeks, providing them with new suits, cash and the opportunity to live like fighting cocks, even showing themselves in the private box of the Attorney General at the Italian Opera House. We captured the Deane Park gamekeeper and kept him at the Anchor where he hid from the Blues, most of the time in the chimney, and on polling day itself we took a cattle drover called Stephen Scott, drunk to the point of insensibility, to stay at the Beehive in Denne Road until he came to his senses enough to vote.

It was the only occasion in Horsham electioneering, as I recall, that a licensed beer house was used for the purpose of *sobering* someone!

And so it went on. We served raw brandy in wine glasses and tumblers. Horsham was kept in a state of continual turmoil, a perpetual whirl of excitement and strong drink. Butchers thrust joints of meat into passing baskets, confident they would get paid elsewhere; new hats were provided where old ones had been bashed in; traps were hired to bring in country voters who were given drink, furnished with eatables and sent home again replete. We spent £350 on blue ribbons. Livestock was provided; horses and cattle were used to obtain votes and even mortgages were paid off where a vote could be obtained. Liquor, house repairs, holidays and small sums of money were dispensed, but as polling day grew close the sums rose from £1 or £2, to £5 and £20, often to the same voters who had already been paid but were in need of 'refreshers'.

I was finally called upon to sit in a private room at the Crown with bags of gold as persuaders.

And of course we had one other advantage over Fitzgerald: the Attorney General was in an eminent position for the distribution of official favours to those who had an eye to business. Sir John Jervis proved to be an excellent promiser: a job as postmaster here, a position in the Excise there; many offices were agreed upon.

But as Charlie Feist regularly reported to us as a double agent, openly working for Fitzgerald but secretly being paid by us, the Pinks also were spending freely, bribing widely, threatening effectively so that by the end of May the town was knee-deep in liquor and every form of blandishment, bribe and menace that could apply, was used. The town was up to its armpits in bribery and corruption and alarmingly Charlie Feist was reporting that each day there were only a handful of votes between the parties.

I calculated that by the end of my campaign I had employed over ninety individuals in the business and it was reported that the costs heaped upon Fitzgerald in his campaign exceeded £6,000. Our expenditure, I may add, was never announced, and indeed, never openly admitted.

So we finally came to nomination day. I was exhausted but the town was agog with excitement, with flags and ribbons flying everywhere. The candidates paraded at nine o'clock in the morning. Both marched around the town, Fitzgerald, preceded by the Horsham band, while we followed behind the band from Dorking, which was bigger, noisier and more expensive. At ten o'clock in the Market Square we climbed the hustings, a wooden structure with a canvas awning erected outside the Town Hall. The Under-Sheriff read out the nominations. Fitzgerald and young Jervis each delivered a prepared speech and the moment came: the Under-Sheriff called to the assembled, cheering crowd, demanded a show of hands from those entitled to vote.

And to an immense roar of approval and a storm of

disapproving catcalls John Jervis was declared duly elected.

It was not the finale, of course.

A poll was called for by Fitzgerald amid a storm of cheering, hissing and booing and then the entire population of the town and numerous visitors from the outlying area returned to their horseplay, jeering, drinking and fighting. Captain Thomas knocked down Constable Green again, tubs of beer were brought out onto the gaol green, the tide of liquor and gold flowed once more and that evening we held our final 'big do' at the Anchor, with John Jervis in the chair and me acting as vice chairman. We ended the dinner with champagne and cigars.

As the party broke up I saw Charlie Feist skulking near the doors. He gestured towards a private room. I followed him into the room, reluctantly.

'Mr Fitzgerald reckons he needs only six votes to win,' he muttered to me from behind his hand, even though no one was in earshot. 'He's offering me £1,000 to find them.'

I knew a villain when I saw one. I shook my head. 'I can pay you £300, not a penny more.'

Our double agent stuck out a hand. I took it with a taste of mud in my mouth: I knew I was being gulled, but it was Jervis's money, after all.

So, next day, under a louring sky the final act of the drama was played out. Rotten eggs and bags of flour sweetened and ornamented both the hustings and their occupants. Substantial breakfasts were consumed, victuals and drinks supplied in astonishing amounts and most voters seemed to be hiccupping their way to declarations for one or the other of the candidates. Some Pink voters were carried forward on boards by their purchasers; some fell down immediately after voting and though I knew we were leading the poll all day, it was never by more than twelve votes.

And there was a free fight, of course; equally inevitably, a major participant was Captain Thomas with his usual opponent, Constable Green. The skirmish only ended when the Under-Sheriff himself marched in, grabbed Captain Thomas and threatened him with legal proceedings.

But Charlie Feist proved his mettle for once. He approached Market Square in a gig, displaying a prominent Pink Fitzgerald ribbon in his hat but when asked the question by the Returning Officer, 'For whom do you vote?' he turned to the crowd, ripped off his pink ribbon, tore open his jacket and exposed a blue ribbon pinned to his shirt. 'I have Pink outside,' he shouted, 'but I have Blue nearest my heart and I vote for Mr Jervis!'

The unprincipled rogue must really have had a simmering resentment against Fitzgerald's agent in a dispute over a cart, after all.

And when the clock struck four it was found we, the Blues, had polled one hundred and sixty-four votes. Fitzgerald had amassed one hundred and fifty-three Pink votes.

We had won.

I need not describe the carousing that followed.

It wasn't the end for Captain William Lanham Thomas, of course. On the 21 August he appeared at Petty and Quarter sessions: he was fined £2 for assaulting Police Constable Richard Green at the Anchor on the 17 June. For two further assaults on the same constable on Polling Day he was sentenced to one day's imprisonment and fined £5 and costs. And he, along with Messrs Honeywood, Blackiston, Beck, Clark, Boxall, Lambert and Mills were summoned for unlawfully and riotously assembling and meeting together and entering the dwelling house of William Robert Seymour Fitzgerald and making a great noise, riot and disturbance and affray therein. The charge was dismissed upon their making an ample apology and donating £20 to charities. My own presence on the occasion was not mentioned—after the discreet intervention of the Attorney General.

Captain Thomas's troubles as far as the Horsham election was concerned were ended.

But my involvement was far from over, and a scandal was looming large.

4

My forensic experience at election committees meant that I was not surprised, some days later, when I heard that Fitzgerald had decided to try to unseat young Jervis. The grounds on which his supporters intended to proceed were that the elected candidate had indulged in bribery and corruption!

I met Sir John Jervis in his chambers. I was shocked by his appearance; he did not look well. His face seemed thinner, a racking cough disturbed him constantly and he seemed to have lost some of his self-assurance. He was not long for this life, of course, though I was unaware of that at that particular time.

'I am not unduly disturbed at the threat of this petition, James,' he remarked with a slight smile. 'They can hardly hope to deprive John of the fruits of his victory by proving his success at methods which they themselves had tried and failed.'

I readily agreed with that view.

'On the other hand there are other considerations to take into account. Have you seen the report in the *Sussex Advertiser*?'

I had not. The Attorney General handed me the cutting he had taken from the newspaper. I can quote it still, from memory:

'It has been most notorious that the most open and barefaced corruption existed on both sides at the recent Horsham election.

There was no concealment, no disguise. It was universally known
that there existed no distinctive pre-eminence of vice on either
side. And it is reported to our correspondent that it is universally
believed that the financial support for the election of Mr Jervis was
provided by the Treasury itself, to the extent even of £8,000. . . .'

I looked up at Sir John. His eyes were fixed on me: he did
not need to tell me how disturbed he was by the allegation of
corruption on the part of the Government itself, and the tarring of
his own reputation as Attorney General.

'Newspaper talk,' I muttered unconvincingly.

He shrugged, raising his lean shoulder in contempt. 'But
damaging. It cannot be allowed to go on. We have made
representations to Mr Fitzgerald. It has been made clear to him that
he would fail in a petition because of his own . . . responsibility for
what went on. He has seen the wisdom of the advice. It has been
agreed that he will not contest John's election. But . . .' he coughed
into his handkerchief; it was a raw, throat-raking dry sound, 'but,
his stepping back does not mean that his supporters will follow his
lead.'

I waited, thinking. He was right, of course. If the Pinks could
find someone, a nonentity perhaps who was untainted by what
had gone on at Horsham, embarrassment for all might follow. And
Lord George Bentinck, in his malice, would no doubt be prepared
to fund the proceedings.

'Mr Padwick, Mr Fitzgerald's agent, has been in touch. He tells
me a certain Mr Newmarch is prepared to bring the petition.
However . . . Mr Padwick proposes a meeting.' He paused, eyed me
carefully as he coughed into his handkerchief. 'This is no reflection
upon your efforts, James, and I remain indebted to you. But with
the rumours that are now circulating in the coffee houses, and the
Government's delicate position . . . I think my son's interests must
be disregarded for the moment. Mr Padwick has a proposition to

make which will relieve both sides of anxiety. You would do me a
great service if you would be so kind as to meet Padwick and . . .
discuss financial matters.'

'As your agent, to reach a compromise, Sir John?'

He hesitated. 'An agent—'

I held up a warning hand. 'No, on second thoughts, perhaps we
should not formally discuss an *agency*. It might be better if I were
able to act freely . . . not *exactly* on your behalf.'

I don't know if he then knew what I had in mind: he had a keen
legal intellect, but he had not been schooled in the world of the
Old Bailey. Because it's all about how you present a case, how you
bamboozle the other side, how you *seem* to make promises but in
fact do not do so. . . .

I met Mr Padwick the next day, when he consented to join me at
The Nunnery for a private discussion.

I was already aware that Mr Fitzgerald's agent held no great
love for me: he had been irritated from the beginning of the
campaign by the efficacy of our methods and the speed in which
we adjusted our strategies. Now, refusing the offer of a glass and a
cigar, he was inclined to move straight to business as he sat there
before me, legs wide apart, hands folded over his extensive belly,
bald head shining in the afternoon sun that streamed in through
the window.

'So, Mr James, you have agreed this meeting to discuss the
election petition we intend to bring.'

'That is so. Though, as an experienced advocate at election
committees, I would advise that you will have little chance of
success.'

Padwick permitted himself a wintry solicitor smile. 'That's as
may be. If we present the petition in the name of the candidate—'

'You will be laughed out of the committee room. Mr Fitzgerald
would be complaining of practices in which he himself indulged.'

Padwick's eyes were stony. 'That is not our intention. A

supporter of the candidate, Mr Newmarch, will present the petition—'

'Which, even if it succeeded in unseating Mr Jervis could not result in the election of Mr Fitzgerald, against whom our side would proffer similar charges.' I paused. 'So where is the advantage to either?'

'Ah. But you disregard the other matter.'

'Which is?'

'The illegal use of Government funds to support the candidature of Mr Jervis.'

He had read the *Sussex Advertiser*. I suspected he had even placed the story there. 'Can you prove the use of Government funds?' I demanded.

He smiled a fat, confident, self-satisfied smile. 'Would we need to? The embarrassment would be huge for the Attorney General; the Government would find mud sticking. The consequences for the party would be unimaginable.'

We both fell silent, watching each other like sparring fighting cocks. At last, almost diffidently, I said, 'I believe we could find a way out of this ... impasse. I have considerable experience in these matters and am prepared to admit that an election committee could find both parties equally to blame if charges of bribery and corruption were to be brought. That would be in the interests of neither your candidate nor Mr Jervis. However, if the charges brought were to be reduced to, say, *treating*, I think that, in the circumstances, we would be prepared to accept the possible unseating of the Attorney General's son.'

A gleam of satisfied triumph appeared in Padwick's cold eyes. 'If we confine the charge to mere treating, and raise no issue of Treasury financial support, your side would raise no defence?'

I hesitated, but knew that we had no choice, really: the position of the Attorney General was too delicate. His son would have to wait another day to make his appearance in the House of

Commons. 'We would raise no defence.'

Padwick nodded slowly. I waited. At last, he smoothed one hand over his bald pate, tugged at his side-whiskers and murmured, 'You act as agent for Sir John in this matter, I take it.'

I stared at him, said nothing, but nodded almost imperceptibly.

'Our side has been put to considerable expense.' He stared at me coldly, now convinced that he had the upper hand. 'Sir John has much to lose, not least his reputation and that of the Government. Whereas on our side, it is merely a matter of *money* rather than honour. So, Mr James, I am instructed by Mr Fitzgerald that our side will be prepared to confine our charges at the hearing next week to *treating* merely, on condition that your candidate makes no defence to the charge and gives up the seat.' He paused. 'And furthermore we would require that Mr Jervis—or preferably Sir John Jervis himself—shall pay the costs of the petition.'

His smile hardened. 'In this way the name of the Attorney General will not be directly connected with charges of bribery and corruption, he will be relieved from a very unpleasant and undignified position and the Treasury itself will not be drawn into a damaging financial dispute with serious political connotations.'

I nodded, seeming to acquiesce. 'You speak of the costs of the petition—'

'We would estimate these to be in the nature of £1,500,' Padwick said blandly and flicked some non-existent fluff from the shoulder of his coat.

I watched specks of dust dance in the shafts of sunlight through the window and considered the oft-repeated claim that attorneys were often no better than highwaymen but I retained the solemn expression that befitted the occasion, and my situation. At last I sighed, as though in defeat. 'Mr Padwick,' I said, 'in the capacity as agent of Sir John Jervis I am able to say that I believe we are in agreement. You will water down the charge, we will not defend the claim of treating and Mr Jervis will relinquish the seat. And

Sir John will make a payment to your office sufficient to cover the costs of the petition—'

'One thousand five hundred pounds,' Padwick intervened smugly.

'Agreed.'

Padwick rose and extended his hand. I took it: his grasp was limp and damp. 'It is a pleasure to deal with gentlemen,' he said, 'in a gentlemanly fashion.'

And so, the following week, the election committee had little to do. The petition was presented on the grounds of treating; no defence was raised; and the declaration was made: John Jervis was to relinquish the seat at Horsham.

But Fitzgerald, of course, was not automatically given the seat. That worthy gentleman went down on the last London train that same day and entered Horsham in triumph preceded by the town band and with his supporters celebrated at the Kings Head. But it was all show and *bravado*.

The Sussex Advertiser reported the events:

'Why did not Mr Fitzgerald claim the seat for Horsham when his opponent had been unseated? You know well! If he had claimed the seat his return would have been petitioned against too . . . and he would have been held up to the laughter and contempt of mankind. . . .'

I duly reported to Sir John Jervis and advised him of the next steps we should take. Accordingly, a few days later when Padwick presented his bill for £1,500 it was rejected politely by the Attorney General.

The furious solicitor stormed around to my chambers in Inner Temple Lane. Waving Sir John's refusal letter he shouted, 'The Attorney General refuses to pay! You made a fool of me, Mr James! Sir John denies that he ever instructed you as his agent in this matter! You took the task on yourself, without reference to him! It's to you now, sir, that I turn to demand redress.'

I leaned back in my chair, folded my hands over my waistcoat and smiled at the plump, flustered solicitor.

'Redress? In what matter?'

'The agreed costs of the election petition!' he spluttered. 'The money you promised me would be paid—'

'I promised? You are mistaken, Mr Padwick, I made no such promise *in my behalf*!'

'I'll have satisfaction of you, sir, I shall take the matter to court—'

'Where your suit will fail, my legal friend.'

'Sir John refuses to pay—'

'Because he authorized no such promise.'

'So *you* must pay!'

I spread my hands wide, mockingly helpless. 'But you must know the law, Mr Padwick. I made no such promise *in my own name*. You were aware at all points that I was acting as an agent for Sir John . . . unfortunately, unauthorized, but there you are! If Sir John denies liability, how can you fix liability on me? I made no promise that I would pay *in person*. You knew that. How could you then persuade a court otherwise?' I smiled. 'I regret, Mr Padwick, there will be no £1,500 forthcoming.'

There was a long silence, broken only by the harsh, frustrated breathing of the infuriated, outwitted solicitor. At last he turned away, pausing only to stop at the doorway to snarl over his shoulder, 'You sir, you are a *rogue*!'

I dismissed him from my chambers with a disdainful flick of the hand. 'I fear, Mr Padwick, that of rogues at Horsham there were a very great number.'

Rogues. It was only a short time later while at the Nottingham Assizes, that I received the request from Lewis Goodman, demanding that I attend a meeting at the hostelry near Welbeck

Abbey. There, I found myself in the presence of four men, who my old enemy, Sir George Bentinck, immediately described in the same manner. Rogues.

A meeting of rogues, on the day that he came to his mysterious end.

PART THREE

1

It's a curious thing that when a man of notability dies a torrent of words will gush forth about him, mostly exaggeration, much ill-informed, and a great part wishful memories endowing an individual in death with qualities he never actually possessed in life.

Such was certainly the case with my bitter enemy, Lord George Bentinck, after his demise near the Abbey Inn.

He was the younger son of the Duke of Portland and had devoted his young adulthood to sporting pursuits including an overwhelming passion for horse racing. Although he had been an MP since 1828 he had displayed no great interest in politics until he came out as an opponent of Peel's Corn Laws, the dispute that split the Tory Party and sent it into the wilderness of Opposition. After his intervention—the first time Bentinck had spoken in Parliament in eighteen years—Sir Robert Peel's administration ended and in due course Bentinck emerged as Leader of the Opposition in the Commons.

Now, after his death, the journals were filled with glowing accounts of his greatness, his perspicacity, his unflinching courage in debate, his gargantuan efforts in the cleansing of the Augean Stables of the racing fraternity and, according to his unctuous admirer Disraeli, his indomitable support for all that was decent and honourable in public life. I could have disputed with Disraeli on that account.

It was only later that a more reflective view began to appear, not least when his cousin and diarist Charles Greville wrote of Bentinck's meanness, avarice, vicious hounding of men with whom he disagreed and long-lived malicious persecution of those he felt were his enemies. This was more like the man I knew, and heartily disliked.

In my estimation and experience Lord George had been an arrogant mean-spirited liar, a hypocrite and a cheat: his greatest quality in my view was that he was quite the best hater I ever came across. And it was well enough known that he held a bitter dislike of me and my doings. I had first incurred his ire in the *Running Rein* trial; later I had disgraced and mocked his aristocratic friend Lord Huntingtower in the courtroom and I had bested his minion Fitzgerald in the Horsham by-election; on the other hand Bentinck's only successful recourse, to his intense frustration, had been to blackball me at the Carlton Club—a disappointment which I had turned aside by becoming a Radical and joining the Reform Club instead, and to his fury had since been enjoying the patronage of his political opponents, Sir John Jervis and Viscount Palmerston.

So, having such a notable enemy, it was not unexpected that I should be questioned, eventually, about the matter and manner of his death. The task fell to another of my *bêtes noirs*, Inspector Redwood of the Metropolitan Detective Squad.

The narrow-eyed, lean-visaged detective officer cornered me some three weeks after Bentinck's death. As I came out of a hearing in the Court of Exchequer there he stood, frock-coated, his black-varnished hat in his hand as he waited in the echoing Great Hall, among the scurrying clerks, sellers of scrip, nervous witnesses and urgent barristers, and he asked me politely if he might be granted the privilege of a few words. I was not pleased, and was tempted to deny him the pleasure on the ground of pressing engagements elsewhere, but on reflection I thought it best to give him a few minutes.

He gestured me to a bench against the wall. We sat side by side, subjected to occasional curious glances from passing lawyers of my acquaintance.

'Well, Redwood, what is it?' I growled unhappily.

Redwood smiled faintly, took out his notebook, glanced at it briefly and then began. 'I have been entrusted by the Commissioner with the handling of inquiries into the unhappy demise of Lord George Bentinck some weeks ago.'

I took a deep breath to calm my nerves. 'My understanding is that he died of a heart attack.'

Redwood nodded sagely. 'That is what has been put about by the family. But privately, between you and me, Mr James, there are still questions to be asked, avenues to be investigated, tracks to be pursued in considering the circumstances surrounding his death. There are certain mysteries. . . .'

He waited briefly but I made no response so he went on.

'We have fairly full information about the events of that unhappy day near Welbeck Abbey, his ancestral home. Indeed, the facts are well known; the information has appeared in the newspapers. On the fatal day, Lord George wrote three letters after breakfast—they are of no consequence—and then announced he intended to visit Lord Manvers at Thoresby, making his way there on foot. A valet was despatched to Thoresby that afternoon with a trap, preceding him, to be available for his return. Lord George left Welbeck Abbey at a little after four in the afternoon.'

'I read an account of all this in *The Times*,' I muttered, but my pulse was beginning to race.

'There were few sightings of his lordship after he began his walk, though he was seen near the ancient Abbey. At about half past four, some woodmen saw him leaning against a gate, apparently reading. At first they thought it was his brother, Lord

Titchfield, but they then realized that it was, in fact, Lord George. They did not address him; as they passed by he ignored them, appearing deep in thought.'

'What has this got to do with me?' I demanded suddenly.

Inspector Redwood had the temerity to smile at me. 'Ah, well, Mr James, it is a well-attested fact that Lord George held certain strong views about you.'

'Among many others,' I growled, irritated.

'And we are speaking to others apart from you, Mr James,' Redwood replied blandly. 'But in view of the bad blood between you, I consider it wise that we should talk. You will have read the reports and you will be aware that the body of Lord George was found early on the Monday morning. He had not appeared at the home of Lord Manvers, and after waiting until evening the valet had returned alone in the trap. So it was only after some hours that the alarm was raised, a search of the surrounding area was instigated and the body was found near the footpath leading to the ruined Abbey.'

I was having difficulty breathing. I glanced around at the passing groups: litigants, lawyers, pamphlet hawkers, sellers of pies. 'You seem to be treating this as a murder inquiry, but I have read that there were no signs of violence on his corpse,' I said savagely.

'No one has yet mentioned murder, Mr James! But as to signs of violence, that is so. Apart from one large bruise, high on the chest,' Redwood replied, watching me keenly. 'And I may say the post mortem investigation proved . . . inconclusive.'

'I still don't know why you're talking to me. How can I help you in this business?'

'Well, sir, a number of rumours have been circulating since his lordship's death. Regarding quarrels he has had recently—'

'Of which there have been a large number, I've no doubt,' I muttered.

'We have already investigated a rumoured dispute he had with his elder brother, the Marquis of Titchfield—'

I had already picked up on that one: Charlie Wilkins, who had a fine ear for gossip, had recently told me the dispute concerned a certain lady, a Miss Barkley. She took the Marquis to court, incidentally, a year later, averring he had gone through a ceremony of marriage with her, he using the pseudonym Druce. But that's by the way. Redwood was waiting for my reaction. I kept my own counsel.

Redwood sighed. 'And there is the quarrel he has of long standing with Mr Greville, his cousin. He has been interviewed. There have been others I have had discussions with, not least among the racing fraternity, John Day, Squire Osbaldeston—'

'With whom he once fought a duel,' I muttered.

'Quite so and there are others but . . . ah . . . it was during such discussions that *your* name came up again.'

'Lord George made no secret of his views as far as I was concerned.'

'You saw him as an enemy?'

'He saw me as one.'

'And your view of the matter?'

'I have no reason to answer that question.'

Inspector Redwood was not put out of countenance. He nodded, smiled again, baring his yellowing teeth. He had shaven badly that morning; he scratched the dark stubble on his cheek with a thoughtful finger. 'But as a matter of interest, what were you doing that Sunday, Mr James, the afternoon Lord George died?'

I turned my head to glare at him. 'I consider it none of your business, Redwood, but if you must know, I was working at my chambers in Inner Temple Lane.'

His tone was lugubrious. 'But according to my information, gleaned from the newspapers, you were attending the Assizes at Nottingham that week. You were briefed on the matter of a certain

Drury Lane actress claiming breach of promise by a certain well-respected member of the House of Lords—'

'The matter was concluded on Saturday. Successfully. I immediately returned to London,' I lied.

'I see. . . . And on the Sunday, in your chambers, you were alone?'

'Naturally.'

'So there is no corroboration—'

'I see no need for you to seek any,' I snapped.

'So it would have been impossible for you to be anywhere near the footpath where the *accident* occurred, that day?'

'For what purpose would I be there?' I countered.

I had already given him the lie; it would be his problem to find me out in that lie. Certainly, none of the men who really knew of my whereabouts that day would be inclined to talk to the police. I felt on safe ground, but nevertheless I was trembling.

Redwood did not seem disturbed, but I felt he was aware of my little evasions. He merely smiled again, in that wolfish way he had, sat in quiet contemplation for a short while then folded his notebook into his pocket and stood up. His tone was falsely apologetic. 'It's merely there have been rumours, and one must follow all lines of inquiry. But I am grateful for your assurances. Should any further questions be necessary I know your address in chambers. Good day to you, Mr James.'

I did not rise with him, nor follow him immediately from the Great Hall. My thighs were twitching, and I was weak at the knees. It was several minutes before I regained control of myself and on quivering limbs made my way back to Inner Temple Lane.

Ah, yes, I'm not surprised you ask me again about that meeting at the Abbey Hotel, and the men I met there that day. Who were they? Well, let me say that when Bentinck burst in on us, he was correct in his description of them as rogues. I've told you that one was a man I had represented already: Edward Agar. At Lewis

Goodman's behest I had got him off a charge of passing forged notes, as I have already related. He walked free on that day, but whether or not the notes had been planted on him by the police on that occasion, matters little: he really *did* make a living as a forger of banknotes. An activity for which he paid the penalty, eventually. Transportation for fourteen years.

Agar was also a known associate of James Townshend Saward, who was seated beside him that day at the Abbey Inn. At that time I knew only that Saward was a barrister who had been called to the Inner Temple about 1840, I believe. He had chambers close to mine in Inner Temple Lane, but appeared rarely in the courts. Much later I learned that he had always been more proficient with the forger's pen than the practice of the law: indeed, he was known among the criminal fraternity by the sobriquet of Jem the Penman, and he and Agar worked together for some years stealing blank cheques and presenting them for payment with forged signatures. When things got too hot for them in London they removed their predations to the south coast and elsewhere in the provinces. Saward was caught passing forged cheques at Great Yarmouth some years later. He faced his trial at the Old Bailey in 1857, and was transported to Australia for fourteen years, shortly before Agar.

Lewis Goodman had called me to the meeting. I have already told you about him: a person with wide criminal connections, a rogue who held me in a tight financial grip, a night house owner, a member of the swell mob, a man to be feared. The last person present that afternoon was the banker and Member of Parliament, John Sadleir. I'll tell you more of him later because he was to play another important role in my rise—and my downfall. . . .

Yes, yes, you're right to upbraid me! I've lost my drift again. Where was I?

Ah, yes. The Horsham by-election. It was over, and young Jervis had triumphed, albeit briefly, and his success had been due to my considerable exertions. His father, the Attorney General, had good reason to be grateful to me, not merely because of my activities as his son's election agent—unsuccessful though they might have been in the end—but also for the manner, at the cost of my own reputation, that I had salvaged his from the taint of corruption.

I have said that Sir John was a good promiser. And in that he showed himself true to me. When the noise and chatter over Horsham had died down he showed himself true to his word: I was gazetted by the Lord Chancellor as one of Her Majesty's Counsel. I took silk, had become a senior practitioner at the Bar, and was now entitled to have the letters QC after my name with a consequent considerable rise in fees. But I had not entirely escaped the echoes of the business at Horsham.

The fact is, as a member of the Inner Temple I would have rightly and reasonably expected, upon my elevation to Queen's Counsel, to be automatically elected as a Bencher of my Inn—that is, one of the senior members responsible for conduct of the Inn, as was Charlie Wilkins, already at Serjeants' Inn. This automatic elevation was undertaken by a vote of the already elected Benchers. And it was normally a matter of formality only. But to my fury and chagrin I was not elected. I was blackballed, as I had been at the Carlton Club election years earlier.

Thus, I had the doubtful honour of being the first Queen's Counsel ever to fail election as a Bencher of his Inn.

I was humiliated, of course, and furious. But it was my old friend Charlie Wilkins who explained it to me. We sat in Evans's that evening, before the really raucous singing had started, and, tugging at his luxuriant side whiskers in a somewhat embarrassed fashion, Charlie said, 'You've made too many enemies, James, that's the plain truth of it.'

'What's that supposed to mean?' I demanded truculently.

'You're too controversial . . . and too successful as well, if the truth be known. And then there's your Radical views. The Benchers are Tories to a man. Oh, yes, the Old Bailey judges like you—they enjoy your quips and your rhetoric— but there are others who deem you too flippant, if you know what I mean. A capital man to a jury, yes, but sometimes it puts the noses of your opponents out of joint. And then there's the business of Horsham. . . .'

'My agency at Horsham has nothing to do with the Benchers of my Inn!' I snapped. 'It was beyond their jurisdiction, a private matter and—'

'I agree, my friend, but it ain't about *jurisdiction,* is it? It's about emotions, feelings of moral panic, their sense of probity—'

'*Probity!*' I exploded. 'What did I do at Horsham that the other side didn't do—if not as efficiently?'

'But that's part of the problem,' Wilkins explained patiently, his big, beefy, restraining hand on my arm. 'They saw what you did, and muttered about it in the Inn, and to top it all there was the sleight of hand you displayed with that rogue Padwick.' He chuckled. 'A master stroke, if I may say so, protecting Sir John Jervis that way. But to some of the aristocratic noses on the Bench it was all a little too . . . clever.'

The *Judge and Jury* skit was just starting up and 'Chief Baron' Renton was beginning his salacious routine. I was hardly aware of the mock trial he conducted as I sat there fuming with a brandy and water on the table before me. I had my own personal trials to mull over in discontent.

'Anyway, James,' said Wilkins, patting my knee, 'so you're not a Bencher. It's an insult—the first QC ever to be refused election at his Inn—but it's not important, not where it counts. It ain't going to affect your professional career!'

And Charlie was right. It was a snub by my peers, it was an insult, but I still had the support of Cockburn, Sir John Jervis and Viscount Palmerston. The Treasury briefs continued to pour in; as a QC I was able to command higher fees and I found myself soon enough alongside Alexander Cockburn again. We formed an effective partnership, and when Sir John Jervis suddenly died and

Cockburn took his place as Attorney General, I became Cockburn's right-hand man in the handling of important Treasury briefs.

That was how I came to be beside him in the most sensational murder prosecution of the age. Unfortunately, once again, it raised considerable controversy.

And I was mired in the middle of it.

2

Although I had largely set my back on Basinghall Street Bankruptcy Court I was still in regular receipt of briefs that called for my experience in financial matters, and it was one of these that led me into the biggest criminal trial of the decade. It was my financial acumen and experience of bankruptcy hearings that first brought me face to face with the fraudulent surgeon, rogue and horse-fancier Billy Palmer.

I had already used Ben Gully over a delicate matter that involved some detective work into the activities of Lord Cardigan—you'll recall him, the numb-skulled hero of the charge of the Light Brigade—and a certain lady of quality who was accustomed to welcoming the gallant cavalryman to her drawing room on afternoons when her husband was at his club. When the case later came on—a crim.con. action—Gully's evidence as to what went on between the pair, astride her ladyship's settee, while Gully was ensconced underneath the same item of furniture, caused a week-long sensation in the press. We met regularly, Gully and I, to exchange information and when I asked him to provide me with details regarding Billy Palmer it was at our usual meeting place: Stunning Sam's in Panton Street.

Stunning Sam's.

Ahhh. . . . The name brings back memories. I might mention

that my first personal acquaintance with the clap was the result of an encounter at Stunning Sam's. The donor in question was a tall, blonde young lady who went by the name of Sovrina and claimed to be Russian, of noble extraction, naturally. Her speciality was that she could unbreech you with a few flicks of the wrist, and then, while your ankles were still encumbered Sovrina, dressed only in highly polished leather boots, would grab you around the neck, climb aboard with her long legs wrapped around your hips, and after she'd wriggled around somewhat to obtain the necessary docking, she'd apply a light riding whip to your buttocks and persuade you to stagger around the room. Quite stimulating, really. As you lurched around in this hobbled fashion she'd call out *'Avanti! Avanti!'* Although she persisted in claiming she was Russian, it would seem Italian was her preferred language of passion.

I'm not sure what finally happened to her. Went to France I believe, married a count. But then, every other Frenchman I've met since the end of the Revolution has claimed to be a count. As most upper class whores have claimed to be of noble Russian extraction.

But all that's neither here nor there.

Stunning Sam. He was an amiable enough fellow, and his nickname certainly did not arise as a consequence of a handsome appearance: he had a shaven head, lantern jaw, nose broken in several places, knuckles like paving bricks. But I never made inquiry as to the origins of his sobriquet. I felt to do so might be unwise, and I'd learn more than I wished. I suspected it had something to do with the cudgel he kept behind the bar, always available to settle drunken disputes in his presence. But his establishment in Panton Street was a well-known location for cigars, chops, drink and varied entertainment in a few upstairs rooms where one could be accommodated with young ladies. Not the *habituées* of the Haymarket, or the dollymops of Leicester Square. No, more discreet, a little refined, a lady you could have conversation with, if that was your intention. With Sovrina, of course, the intention was to hear her expound her limited vocabulary of Italian while demonstrating her ability as a horsewoman.

Anyway, as I was saying, Stunning Sam's was the particular establishment at which I usually met Ben Gully, out of sentiment I suppose. Memories of Sovrina, and the discomforts she visited upon me later. . . .

I entered the narrow doorway and walked through the dim, familiar passageway until it opened out into the saloon: a scattering of high-backed Coburg chairs, a haze of cigar smoke, sporting prints yellowing on the walls, dark-panelled corners protected by wooden screens, the odours of stale ale and discreet sex. I sat down near one of the grimy, diamond-paned windows, called for a brandy and water and awaited Ben Gully's arrival. I had had a good morning that day: success in a fifty guinea brief. I was prepared to relax for an hour.

I could tell by the look on Ben's battered features when he came in that he didn't entirely approve of my choice of meeting place. He looked around him, his mouth twisting. 'You know Stunning Sam's not the owner here,' Ben muttered, controlling his wandering eye. 'He fronts for Lewis Goodman.'

'Goodman doesn't seem to be much in evidence these days,' I observed.

Ben nodded. 'The story is, he's gone to France because of his daughter. Some frog's got her in the family way—married Army officer, apparently—and Goodman has gone dancing off in a rage to rescue her. Leastways, that's what I hear. But I got my own suspicions. My guess is he's left these shores because he's got other reasons than family: maybe things have been getting too hot for him.'

He was probably right in his surmise. I looked him over. For our meeting Ben had dressed with some care. His frequently rearranged features still betrayed some of the results of the daily vicissitudes of his existence, but he wore a high stock, a sober dark coat with polished bone buttons, and high boots. The nap on his hat was still good, and his stick of dark walnut gleamed with polish. The heavy brass handle told me it was appropriate not just for show: it also provided a useful means of defence. Or, more likely, assault.

I pushed in his direction the mug of porter I had previously ordered and as he sat down I picked up my own brandy and water. 'I haven't seen much of you lately, Ben,' I announced cheerfully. 'And you're looking quite the swell.'

Ben's odd eye swivelled as he took in his surroundings. 'Been out and about.'

'Noon's Folly, for the Bendigo Boy battle?' I hazarded a guess.

Do you follow the practice of the Noble Art, my boy? I guess not, spending so much time at sea. You'll be more familiar with dockside barroom brawls, I imagine. Well, Noon's Folly was one of the best known places for the prize fights, and was located a few miles from Royston where the counties of Cambridge, Suffolk, Essex and Hertfordshire meet. The magistrates were supposed to interfere, of course, to stop the public display of pugilism but in reality they themselves attended in droves, while hoping the fight did not fall within their personal jurisdictions. Ben Caunt had recently battled at Noon's Folly with the Bendigo Boy, over two and a half hours. Ninety-three rounds were fought but constant threats of the police forced them to move from Newport Pagnell, then to Stony Stratford, on to Wheddon Green and finally Lutfield Green. The crowd followed the pugilists over more than thirty miles before the battle was awarded to Bendigo.

Gully grunted and sipped his porter, wiped his mouth with the back of his gnarled-knuckled hand. 'Noon's Folly? No, I been out of town. Up north. On your business, Mr James.'

There was a sourness in his tone. As I believe I've intimated to you before, Ben Gully was a London man: he knew every nook and cranny in the rookeries, every shady waterman along the river, and every sharp who tried the game in the casinos, public houses and dens of ill repute from Stepney to Mill Hill. In the course of his business, he was a frequenter of dark haunts in Wapping, odorous alleys in St Giles and less than respectable locations behind the smart houses in Regent Street. However, I was aware from his expression that a sojourn in the north—or more precisely, the Midlands—was not to his taste.

'So, was your visit productive?' I asked.

He watched me for a little while without answering. Finally, he grimaced and said, 'I went to the races at Chester.'

'Ha! A change of air, but still following the habits of a lifetime. Did you do well?'

'Backed a few. Lost a bit. Won a bit.'

'Chester Races used to be a favourite venue for Lord George Bentinck,' I mused.

Ben eyed me quizzically. 'That gentleman caused you a lot of trouble when he was alive. I consider his death would have been a kind of relief to you, Mr James. . . .' He hesitated, still eyeing me. 'They never did really find out just how it came about, did they? Him dying up near Welbeck Abbey, I mean.'

I shook my head. I had told Ben nothing of the part I had played in Bentinck's demise. I made no reply now.

Ben was silent for a little while, staring at his porter. Then he looked up at me with clouded eyes. 'Anyway, to business. You asked me to make inquiries about the surgeon William Palmer. So I spent a week at the Chester Races. Watching the nags. Making a few contacts. Talking to people. Listening to the chatter. There was a great deal of that. In fact, Mr James, it was the common talk all week. Mr Palmer, he's well known as a regular frequenter of Chester Races.'

'So what is the talk mainly about?'

Gully caressed a bloody nick on his recently shaven jaw. 'First of all, what you asked me to look out for. There's a lot of talk about the winning nag called *Polestar*, owned by the gent called Cook. Him who died in convulsions.'

'You'd better tell me everything you've heard.'

Alexander Cockburn had already received the brief for the prosecution of William Palmer for murder. He had asked me to be at his side, not least because I had already received a different brief in which Palmer was involved. My first contribution was to find out what was not in the instructions received by Cockburn—which was concerned mainly with the death of John Parsons Cook. We had to be ready for anything the defence might throw at us . . . for in my view the case against Palmer was weak.

Cook and Palmer had been at the Shrewsbury races where Cook's horse *Polestar* had won. Cook had been taken ill thereafter, regularly vomiting, managing to keep little down. He was not alone in his suffering: many in the area had been taken ill at that time. Finally, on the Saturday night after Palmer had returned from a visit to London, John Parsons Cook had died, after taking some pills administered by Palmer. Cook's betting book had disappeared, and our brief called upon us to prove that Palmer had poisoned his friend Cook to avoid paying him what was owed to him. But there were too many holes in the case to afford me satisfaction—or belief that we could bring a successful prosecution.

Ben twisted his mouth. He had lost a tooth since last I saw him. I wondered what the other man would have lost. The waiter was at my elbow. He placed the drink in front of me. Ben leaned back in his chair and grimaced. 'Right. Well, first of all, the general conversation concerned *Polestar*. After the nag won last December, someone is supposed to have said to this man Cook, the owner of *Polestar*, he'd be lucky if he lasted the week.'

'Lasted? How do you mean?'

Gully shrugged. 'They didn't really pursue it . . . they just laughed. But then the gossip in the beer tent went on. I picked up all sorts of information. I went into Stafford and made further inquiries to see how far the locals went along with what I'd heard. In fact, the whole place was alive with chatter. Not least how after *Polestar* won, the aforesaid Mr John Parsons Cook, owner of the nag, he turned up his toes.'

'As predicted.'

'But that could just be gossip after the event, Mr James.'

Frowning, I stroked my chin thoughtfully. I stared at Gully. 'There's more, of course.'

'That's right, Mr James.' He took a deep breath. 'From what I heard, Cook picked up nearly a thousand guineas at the course, with more to come, as a result of *Polestar* winning. But when he died, well there was no sign of the cash he must have picked up.'

I had the feeling Ben's account would be lengthy. We were well away from the serving hatch where the waiter obtained the drinks but I was aware of the enticing odours that were wafted from the kitchen, where pork chops were sizzling on the grill. 'I think a couple of chops would go down well,' I suggested quietly. 'And meanwhile, you can tell me about the general *feeling* in Stafford. . . .'

'And Rugeley,' Ben nodded grimly as I placed the orders. He put down his mug and leaned forward, elbows on the table. 'It all circulates around William Palmer. He was a close friend of *Polestar's* owner, Mr John Parsons Cook, and together they went to Chester Races that day. Palmer had a couple of horses running. He lost considerably. And he was with Cook the night the man died. But more than that, from what I've heard in Stafford and Rugeley, this Dr Palmer, well, you might say he's got a bit of history.'

'That's what I need to hear.'

'He's been somewhat embarrassed for some time, by his financial commitments. Unwise investments.' Ben's eyes fixed on me as though to add something about my own position, then flicked away, aware he might be touching on a sore spot. 'William

Palmer's been up to his eyes in debt as the result of spending money at Chester on horses of poor character, and on Liverpool whores of even less.'

'Earnings?'

'Steady,' Ben shrugged. 'But not large. His surgeon's practice in Rugeley is not a flourishing one. And what with knock-kneed horses, cards and women of easy virtue. . . .' He eyed me carefully, uncomfortably aware of my own predilections in those directions. I sipped my brandy and water. The chops were on the way. I waited, but Ben was silent for a little while, brow furrowed.

'This William Palmer, well, it's not just the races and whores. He's got a history that's, shall we say, unfortunate? He was the sixth of seven children: one sister drank herself to death and there's a brother who worked diligently towards the same end, with the assistance of Dr Palmer, it seems. But his early history, well, Dr Palmer has a doting mother, Sarah Palmer. She arranged for him as a young man to be apprenticed to a Liverpool chemist. He wasn't employed there long. He was caught with his fingers in the till but his mother saved him: she's always seen him as the apple of her eye.'

Ben paused, leaned back as a plate of sizzling chops was placed in front of him. He eyed the chops appreciatively. 'Anyway, after the Liverpool incident, gossip reckons she persuaded a surgeon in Rugeley to give the lad a chance. He was took on as apprentice, but after various incidents of fraud, deceit and seduction he was told to leave. He showed up next at Stafford Infirmary. Went on to St Bart's Hospital and finally qualified in 1846, Royal College of Surgeons. By way of a correspondence course—'

'Let me guess, a correspondence course for which he never paid.'

'You guessed right, Mr James.'

In fact it was already in Cockburn's brief. I was beginning to get bored. This was all so petty. I needed more than I had heard so far.

Ben Gully sniffed, scratched his stubbly chin. 'William Palmer then ups and gets married to one Anne Thornton, the daughter of an Army officer. Illegitimate, but she had prospects. On the strength of them prospects Palmer borrowed money and bought himself a couple of nags, which he ran unsuccessfully, in between siring four sons and a daughter on the said Anne Thornton. Five children. . . .' He sniffed. 'The eldest is still alive.'

I picked up the emphasis. I began to feel a slow, familiar cancer of suspicion in my chest. 'The *eldest*? What about the others?'

Ben wiped some ale from his chin. 'Faded away. It's reported Billy Palmer often said he regarded large families as ruinously expensive,' Ben said coolly.

'How did they die?'

'Officially? Convulsions.'

I was silent for a little while. Infant mortality was high. It could be just bad luck, or bad drains. But five out of six? Yet Ben Gully had not finished.

'Some say he used to put poison with a little honey on his finger and let them suck.'

I grunted sourly. 'Gossip?'

Ben Gully shrugged, leaned back and began to attack the plate of crisp pork chops as mine also arrived. He chewed his appreciatively. 'You know, Mr James, you can say this about Stunning Sam, you don't usually get chops liked these in this kind of establishment. . . . Anyway, there's more to this Palmer story. His wife, Anne Thornton as was, like I said, she had prospects.'

'How much?'

'She expected to get twelve thousand on her mother's death. So it seems William Palmer invited the old lady to come for a holiday. She went to stay with them at Palmer's house in Rugeley.'

'And?'

''The old lady got took ill, and turned up her toes. Sudden.'

I was getting interested. I ignored my pork chops, while Ben champed at his. 'And what might have been the certified cause of death?'

'Apoplexy.' Ben sighed. 'A lot of chatter, but you know, things are funny in Rugeley and Stafford. In spite of all the murmuring, Palmer's popular there. There's people who say Palmer is much maligned, it's all just malicious gossip about his children and his mother-in-law; but there's others who reckon there's no smoke without fire. Perhaps those he owes money to – you know what I mean. And apart from his family losses, there's others. Palmer was friendly with one Leonard Bladen. They used to go to the races together, regular. They say Palmer borrowed money from Bladen, then Bladen had a big win at Chester, and suddenly he dropped dead about a week later. Strange thing was his widow couldn't lay hands on his betting book.'

'Which would have shown a record of what was owing to him. . . . Palmer was challenged?' I asked.

Ben Gully shook his head. 'Inquiries began to be made. But then they was dropped. Mrs Bladen didn't want to go on with it. Mrs Bladen reckoned Anne Palmer was very kind to her. A close friend. So she let things drop.'

I sipped at my brandy and water thoughtfully. 'All this is just local chatter, of course.'

Ben sighed, as though contemplating the wickedness of Man. 'There's plenty more of it. William Palmer's mother, Sarah Palmer, she had a lover. Name of Jeremiah Smith. It was through him that Palmer negotiated an insurance policy on the life of his own wife. Then guess what? Few weeks later, Palmer's wife died after catching a chill at a concert in Liverpool.' Ben paused, eyeing his rapidly disappearing chop. 'It seems the grieving widower didn't mourn long: he picked up thirteen thousand on that policy. He immediately paid off some debts—and within a month insured his drunken brother's life for another fourteen thousand. This brother, he's a man who would regularly toss off half a tumbler of raw spirits before turning black in the face.'

These were details I needed to know in support of Cockburn's brief. 'You're going to tell me that the brother died?'

Gully nodded. 'Not long after. Palmer sent for an undertaker, ordered a coffin and then coolly telegraphed the clerk of the course at Ludlow to find out where his horse had come in the last race.'

I shook my head in disbelief. 'Did the company pay out the insurance?' I asked incredulously.

'When they discovered Palmer had tried it on with three other assurance companies, they demurred. Palmer didn't fight it. So it seems that particular venture didn't come off. But the story is he then tried to insure an acquaintance of his by the name of Bate. The proposal was refused. That didn't stop our surgeon going along with his friend Cook to the Shrewsbury Handicap where they both had horses running. Cook picked up at least eight hundred on the course and was due to get the balance of two thousand from Tattersall's. Palmer's own horse, *Chicken*, did badly and he lost money. The story is that after the races the two men went back to the Raven Hotel. Cook was took ill that very night.'

I nodded. 'And shortly afterwards, died. This is the charge that's to be brought against Palmer.'

'Will you be able to use the rest? The brother, Anne Palmer, the mother-in-law, the children, the insurance companies—'

'It's background, Ben, background, maybe even idle chatter, but it might be crucial. If we can manage to bring it in.'

I thought hard while Gully chomped his way through the chops, took a hunk of bread and wiped his plate. He looked up inquisitively. 'So what's to happen now, Mr James?'

I smiled. 'First of all, I shall be having a meeting with the remarkable Dr Palmer. Face to face. In a court of law.'

3

The hearing took place at the beginning of January at Westminster. William Palmer was at that time held at Stafford Gaol awaiting trial for the murder of John Parsons Cook and this was the only time that he was allowed outside the building: no doubt he appreciated the opportunity to visit the metropolis, for as I was about to discover he was a cool character, our horse-racing surgeon of Rugeley.

Because of my background and experience in the Bankruptcy Court I was a natural choice as counsel to the moneylender Padstone. The brief informed me that Mr Padstone had made a loan of £2,000 to William Palmer, backed by a bill of exchange, which had apparently been signed by Palmer's mother, the widow Sarah Palmer. Padstone was now seeking to recover the two thousand but he was facing a problem. Sarah Palmer denied that the signature on the bill was hers: it had been forged.

The defence produced Mrs Palmer: she was an elderly, grey-haired but spirited lady, well turned out in the latest fashion and bold and firm in her statements. In my examination I was unable to shake her in her denials: she averred stoutly she had not signed the bill. She was then supported by sworn statements from three of her children, siblings of William Palmer. First there was George who swore the signature was not that of his mother; he was followed by his sister Sarah who swore to the same truth and finally the Reverend Thomas Palmer appeared to say the same thing: as a man of the cloth his evidence was particularly damaging to my client.

For as I had already explained to the moneylender Padstone when he first came to my chambers for advice, if the signature on the bill was indeed forged, the bill was worthless. It would be necessary, therefore, to show that William Palmer had obtained the loan by false pretences and forgery, after which he himself could be charged with repayment of the loan—hence the present proceedings.

Of course I had pressed the mother hard.

'Madam, let us be precise. If this is not your signature, it must be a forgery. Since the loan was made to your son William Palmer, it is clear that he must have signed in your name, in order to obtain this money.'

'That cannot be so,' she averred stoutly. 'My Billy would never seek to rob me so!'

So, inevitably, I needed to have the surgeon himself in the witness box, to challenge him and, if possible, to get him to admit the forgery so redress could be obtained by his duped moneylender. I could see the burly, red-cheeked Mr Padstone leaning forward eagerly, with a hungry, angry look in his eye, when Palmer's name was called and the door to the judge's private room was thrown open.

Mr Padstone was not the only eager face craning to get sight of the notorious witness. Indeed, it was a remarkable day. Since William Palmer's arrest there had been a scramble among his creditors to obtain what money they could from his estate: it might prove more difficult if he was to be hanged. His main assets were lodged in the racehorses he owned: Tattersall's craftily put them up for sale on the very day *Padstone v Palmer* was heard, and the coincidence attracted a large gathering in the auction ring and resulted in excited competitive bidding. Westminster Hall was noisily crowded and the courtroom itself packed with urgent onlookers: demand for tickets of entry had been huge. Everyone wanted to catch a glimpse of the notorious surgeon from Rugeley. A collective sigh arose when he made his dramatic entrance, and the courtroom was then briefly silent as all observed him, coming into the dock in the custody of a large and muscular police officer with a black, bushy moustache.

The man I saw in the witness box was then thirty-one years old but looked older, partly because of his thinning, light brown hair brushed back over his forehead: he was solidly built, broad-shouldered and somewhat bull-necked. He was a little above average height, his complexion was florid, his forehead high and intelligent, and nothing in his calm, confident appearance suggested ferocity or cunning. His hands were small, almost pretty in their whiteness: I had heard he was accustomed to wear wash-leather gloves to maintain their plump softness. Now he stood in the witness box and looked about the court: his glance fastened upon a red-haired young woman seated near the lawyer who was conducting the defence case. I understood later she was one Jane Widnall, with whom, among other ladies of loose morals, he had enjoyed a lengthy relationship. I continued to watch him with interest as he was sworn in. He spoke in a firm, distinct tone, his voice betrayed no hesitation or nervousness and I concluded he was a cool, controlled customer.

Just how cool I was quickly to discover.

I went straight to the point. I handed him the bill of exchange which acknowledged the £2,000 loan.

'Is the signature *William Palmer* as the drawer of this bill in your handwriting?'

He glanced at the document, then looked directly at me. 'Yes, it is.'

'And you applied to Mr Padstone to advance you money on this bill?'

His glance held mine steadily, unmoved. 'I did.'

I smiled. We could immediately proceed to the heart of the matter. 'The signatory to the bill is Sarah Palmer. But your mother, Mrs Sarah Palmer, has sworn she did *not* sign this bill. Did you forge her signature?'

'I did not.'

He was lying, I knew. 'So who *did* write Mrs Sarah Palmer's acceptance on it?'

His eyes remained steady; there was no flicker, no hesitation, no hint of concern in his glance. There was a short pause until at last he replied.

'Anne Palmer.'

A palpable hush settled over the room. Everyone seemed to be holding their breath. I myself was momentarily stunned: the effrontery of the reply staggered me. I hesitated, then asked, '*Anne Palmer*. Who is she?'

Calmly, without emotion William Palmer replied, 'She is now dead'

I struggled to breathe. 'Do you mean, are you telling the court that it was your *wife* who signed . . . *forged* your mother's signature?'

'Yes,' he said, holding my fierce glance with a studied lack of concern.

I bit my lip. The case was sliding away from me; if what the surgeon was stating was true, Padstone's case would collapse in a heap. Manfully, I struggled with the only question left to me. 'You say it was your wife's doing. . . . Did you *see* her write the acceptance, in the name of Sarah Palmer?'

'I did.'

There was no way in which he could be gainsaid. I heard the rustle begin in the courtroom behind me; people sat up, whispered, and a shudder of horror seemed to settle upon all who heard the cold, calculated, heartless tone of the man in the witness box. He had taken the money; he had probably forged the name himself; a straightforward confession of forgery and fraud would have saved his mother's honour. Instead, he was blaming his wife, a woman who could not defend herself—subjecting her name to calumny and leaving Padstone without remedy. The moneylender was outmanoeuvred: he could not sue a dead woman for forgery, could not recover his £2,000.

I turned to look at him. He gaped at me, his florid features paling. I shrugged, then informed the court that I had no recourse other than to retire from the case. As the jury announced in favour of old Mrs Sarah Palmer my client grabbed me by the arm. 'Just half an hour ago, before the trial, I bought two of the doctor's horses at Tattersall's. Near five hundred guineas it cost me! I swear, if I'd known how this case would go I'd never have bought hoof nor hair of that twister's bloodstock!'

As he was escorted from the courtroom Palmer glanced back at me, over his shoulder. A slight smile played across his lips.

As I told the recently promoted Attorney General Alexander Cockburn next day, it was clear we were dealing with a cool, collected villain and rogue who would no doubt be able to twist and turn at every occasion. We would need not merely to be sure of our evidence and witnesses; we would have to anticipate just what defences William Palmer might concoct.

Cockburn was gloomy of countenance. 'We have severe problems with our case as it stands. You're right in your views: the evidence against Palmer—the hard evidence of fact—is slim. I believe you've had your man Gully rooting about in Stafford. Has he found anything we can use?'

I shook my head regretfully. 'Rumours . . . plenty of them. But real facts, no. And there's the matter of local feeling.'

'It's against Palmer?'

'Hardly. It may be surprising, but scarcely any people in the locality believe in his guilt: they discount what they hear; they describe it as malicious gossip. They claim Palmer is a generous, kindly man, and one they respect. So the first of our problems is the raising of a jury . . . unbiased.' I frowned. 'The men and women we place in the jury box, if drawn from Stafford and Rugeley, will probably be strongly on Palmer's side. There's been too much talk—everyone knows what's claimed, and many dispute it.'

'So what do you suggest, James?'

'Move the trial.'

And that's how it came about—for the first time in history a criminal case was moved from the assize court in the area where the alleged crime was committed. The process began when I met Palmer's solicitor Mr John Smith in my chambers, next day.

'Honest John' Smith of Birmingham was a man short of leg, wizened of features, with a pendulous lower lip that quivered when he spoke, but he had wide-spaced, sober eyes and an earnest expression. The sobriquet 'Honest John' was at variance with the general view the public holds of lawyers: honesty and law have never been regarded as natural bedfellows. Perhaps he had earned it by the straightforward manner of his speech.

He began by asking if I would lead for the defence of William Palmer! He half-closed his heavy-lidded eyes thoughtfully, and said, 'I will be straight with you, sir. I have proffered my advice to Dr Palmer, stating quite firmly that the most suitable man in all England to speak on his behalf would be Mr Serjeant Wilkins, in view of the fact that he enjoyed a medical education before taking to the Law.'

My old friend Charlie Wilkins, former strolling player, circus act, itinerant preacher, and, for a while, a practising chemist. I nodded gravely, as Smith went on.

'I confidently expect that Serjeant Wilkins would be able to handle the abstruse medical evidence that is expected to be produced by the prosecution better than any other.' Smith paused, inspected his hands, locked together in his lap. He frowned. 'But I fear that Dr Palmer has other views.'

I made no reply but held the solicitor's glance and waited. John Smith shuffled a little uncomfortably in the chair. 'Dr Palmer is well aware of your reputation in . . . ah . . . sensation cases. Moreover, it seems that when he faced you recently in the matter of the forged endorsements he was . . . ah . . . impressed.'

Impressed the wily Dr Palmer might have been, but I suspected it was because he had also heard other rumours concerning my own personal experiences in the matter of horse racing, ladies of easy virtue, bill discounting and debts.

I was silent for a little while, pretending to consider the matter. After a while I rose, locked my hands behind my back, strolled to the window and looked out towards the Temple Gardens. I did not have an uninterrupted view from my chambers: guttering and the edge of a roof obscured most of the view, though I was able to discern a leaden strip of the Thames and a few scrubby trees above the muddy flats that led down to the Temple landing. After a few minutes' silence, I turned back to the expectant Birmingham solicitor.

'I fear I must decline the brief. I have already been instructed by the Treasury and will represent the Crown, alongside the Attorney General. So I suggest you stick with Serjeant Wilkins. But your visit is opportune: I wanted to see you regarding other matters. I have caused certain inquiries to be made at Rugeley and Stafford.'

Smith's wide-spaced eyes narrowed a little, but he waited in silence.

'I won't dwell upon Dr Palmer's racing losses or the general state of his financial affairs,' I went on smoothly, 'but I would remark upon the noticeable number of deaths among people of his acquaintance, such as his unfortunate children, his mother-in-law, his wife, his brother . . . and there is, of course, the matter of his attempts to insure the lives of most of these adults with at least four separate assurance societies. This . . . ah . . . background has caused considerable comment in the local area.'

'Common gossip can hardly be restrained in matters such as these,' Smith averred tightly.

'That is true,' I admitted. 'But it seems to me to raise a certain problem. The trial will be held at Stafford. From the information I have received, while there are numerous acquaintances of Dr Palmer in Rugeley who will swear to his probity and offer strong support for his defence, the situation is somewhat different in Stafford. There, local feeling is strongly against the good doctor. The gossip swirls around readily; many believe already in the guilt of Dr Palmer on the basis of the old adage that there can be no smoke without fire, and there exists a great deal of, shall we say, prejudgment?'

'The situation is indeed unfortunate,' Smith admitted.

'Particularly since the members of the jury will be drawn from the local area, if the trial is to be heard in Stafford.'

The silence that followed grew. I settled myself back in my chair, steepled my fingers, observed the Birmingham solicitor. At last, with furrowed brow, he sighed. 'I agree, it is possible there will be difficulty with the selection of the jury. Many people are likely to be somewhat prejudiced.'

'Which would suggest to me,' I said carefully, 'that Dr Palmer is unlikely to obtain a fair hearing at Stafford.'

John Smith sniffed, and scratched at his cheek. 'There's not much we can do about that. If we—'

I held up my hand, interrupting him. 'The Crown wants a level playing field,' I lied. 'The concept of a fair trial is deeply entrenched in English Law. The Attorney General and I consider a case could and should be made for the removal of the hearing to a location other than Stafford. On the ground of avoidance of local prejudice.'

I did not mention the prejudice was largely against the Crown prosecution. John Smith stared at me for several long seconds. 'There is no provision in English law—'

'But perhaps there *should* be such provision.'

'That would require an Act of Parliament.' Smith snapped, but there was a light dawning in his eyes.

'Just so.'

'There would hardly be time, even if the Government could be persuaded—'

'Justice should be blind,' I murmured, 'not prejudiced.' I paused. 'And I am assured the Attorney General—and the Government—would not be averse to such a petition.'

Smith took the bait. He was persuaded the prejudice would be against his client: next day, to our delight, he presented the petition, and we achieved our objective in getting a London, rather than a Stafford jury, for shortly after the interview Sir Alexander brought in a bill, which was hastily promulgated as law as Act of Parliament, *19 Vict.cap 16,* to regularize the proceedings.

I had dinner with Lecky Cockburn at the Reform Club, while the draft Act lay before Parliament and informed him of my other anxieties. Over a glass of Madeira he observed me with a cynical glint in his eye. 'So now we know all the rumours about this man Palmer.'

'And I've confronted the man in court. He's a smooth customer.'

'I've gone over the brief thoroughly. It's not one of our firmest and clearest cases. Too many holes. I think, James, we don't have time tonight, for I have a political meeting to attend. But you and I need a conference of war. This Friday I intend going down to my yacht. Perhaps we could meet there?'

'Or after a convivial evening at The Nunnery?'

Cockburn laughed. 'It's a while since I've attended a Cock and Hen occasion. Rusper it is then, and afterwards, on to *The Zouave.'*

I was relieved. I needed to give Cockburn my views regarding what the defence was likely to throw at us.

4

After the ladies had left The Nunnery that afternoon, a sated Cockburn and I settled down to a cigar, and I left a bottle of good brandy at his elbow. He helped himself, sniffed at his glass, gave a slight sigh of appreciation and sipped, holding his head back to allow the taste and aromas to linger on his tongue. Then he looked at me quizzically, and said, 'The trap will be here in a half hour, to take us down to the yacht. Well, James? What do you think?'

We had already had discussions in his chambers on the case for the prosecution of Dr Palmer and we were of a mind. He would be the leader, of course, and as Attorney General, would undertake most of the advocacy. My task was to prepare the medical evidence, drill the seven eminent surgeons in their presentations, and try to outguess the defence in their strategies. We had worked hard at the brief and I had collated the evidence, interviewed the witnesses we expected to call. Now, I stretched out in my chair, brandy glass in one hand, a glowing cigar in the other. 'The medical evidence will be critical, in the minds of the jury.'

'Ah, yes. Led by Professor Taylor.' Cockburn wrinkled his nose in dissatisfaction. 'He worries me.'

'Because of his view regarding the cause of death,' I murmured.

'Exactly that. First of all, after his post mortem examination, Professor Taylor was of the opinion, and has so deposed, that he was convinced Cook had been poisoned by a dose of antimony.'

I sniffed contemptuously. 'The problem with *that* theory is that during the autopsy on John Parsons Cook only one small grain of antimony was found in the internal organs. Not enough to kill. Indeed, it seems most of us at some time or another carry a similar amount inside our gut without any ill effects.'

'At which point,' Cockburn grunted sourly, 'our good professor gives us the opinion that Palmer *could* have poisoned Cook with strychnia, not antimony after all.'

'And the problem with *that*,' I murmured, 'is that no post-mortem evidence of the ingestion of strychnia can be shown.'

Cockburn twisted uneasily in his chair. 'Confound all damned medical men! Why can't they be more precise? It's all very well saying the symptoms attending the death of Cook are *consistent* with strychnine poisoning, but if they can't find a trace of the stuff in the organs, where does that leave us?'

'Dangling in mid-air,' I remarked thoughtfully.

'Where I'd like to see that damned rogue Palmer,' Cockburn snapped viciously.

And I need to make a point here. I had no decided *animus* against Dr Palmer. But Cockburn, he was determined to get a conviction, I knew that. The fact was, Alexander Cockburn was always a vain man, and he liked to win. Moreover, as Attorney General he wanted to maintain his reputation; perhaps more importantly, he was due any day now to expect elevation to the bench, as Lord Chief Justice. The Palmer case was likely to be the last great *cause célèbre* that would fall to him before he became elevated to the bench and he wanted to go out in a blaze of glory. And oddly enough, for all his personal interest in and ability at card-sharping and whoring and impregnating other men's wives, there was a strangely Puritan streak in him. He disliked Palmer in a way I did not: he saw the Rugeley doctor as a rogue, a scamp, a fraudster, a horse-nobbler and a seducer. And he had convinced himself that Palmer was a murderer. I held a somewhat different view: I had met many Palmers in the bankruptcy courts and in fraud and bill-discounting cases. I had personal experience of the wriggling often necessary to fob off one creditor against another. So I had some brotherly feeling for Palmer. And I did not believe he was a killer. On the other hand, I had my professional duty.

'Do you think Professor Taylor's testimony will stand up in court?' he asked abruptly.

I shrugged, sipped my brandy. 'We've got three other eminent professors and three doctors to support him.'

'And the defence have five professors and six doctors directly opposed and willing to affirm Cook died of natural causes. They claim it could have been syphilis or tetanus.'

'It don't come down to numbers,' I said coolly, drawing on my cigar and sending a curl of smoke up the ceiling. I squinted at its coiling perfection before I added, 'And we've got the evidence of Charles Newton.'

'Which we'll go over when we get down to Southampton Water,' Cockburn grunted, stubbing out his cigar. 'The trap is at the door.'

We remained silent as we rattled our way to the coast, each to our own thoughts. I suspect his mind was not distant from mine: we had enjoyed the favours of three ladies that afternoon, bored, complaisant and seeking illicit thrills. Cockburn and I were adept at providing the right kind of table—and bed—for such appetites. As for a couple of days on *The Zouave*, that was not really to my taste. Unlike you, my boy, master mariner that you are, I do not have any trace of the sea in my blood. I knew that Cockburn would not be putting out from his moorings at that time of the year, but he liked to sit on the deck well muffled up against the breeze with a wide brimmed hat on his head to deflect the damp airs. He claimed the sea winds helped clear his head: they caused mine to seize up with migraine. But he was my leader, Attorney General, and in charge of proceedings.

My task was to predict what the defence might raise to foil us in our objective—to see Palmer hang—and find ways in preventing those defence arguments prevailing.

After a fitful night in my rocking cabin and a bracing breakfast on shore at a local inn, the Attorney General and I settled down on the deck of *The Zouave*, brandy and water in hand, and went over what we needed to look out for in the coming trial.

Cockburn sighed. 'Ah, yes, you were saying, the chemist Charles Newton, the man who claims he sold grains of strychnia to Palmer on the night Cook died. Which Palmer then made up into pill form and gave to his unfortunate friend.'

'In other words, the means to an end. Unfortunately, defence counsel will point out that there's no record of the sale in Newton's books,' I murmured.

Cockburn nodded thoughtfully and squinted skywards where a winter sun was part obscured by drifting clouds. 'Newton will swear that he did not record the sale because his employer, Dr Salt, had a long standing feud with Palmer, and had ordered that Newton should not serve Palmer with drugs. Newton didn't want his master to know he had disobeyed him. No, I think we'll be all right there. Newton's evidence will stand up in court.'

'There's some evidence of bad feeling between Newton and Palmer,' I countered.

'I doubt we can contest that. But Newton is likely to be a solid witness: he won't be moved. So, I think we can assume the means for murder were supplied to Palmer. Newton will swear he provided Palmer with the means to kill Cook—'

'Though I'd like to come back to that,' I interrupted.

'. . . And Dr Taylor and his merry medical men will swear that Cook died from strychnine poisoning.'

'Even though they found no strychnia in the organs, and in the first instance Taylor had announced the death was caused by antimony,' I reiterated.

Cockburn grunted dismissively. We remained silent for a little while, each dwelling on our own thoughts. My mind wandered back to the previous evening at The Nunnery, the softness of female thighs and the scent of the woman's hair; I recalled the lusty heaving of her loins against mine, and the delighted groaning during our romp. You know, that idiot William Acton, who wrote that the majority of women are not very much troubled with sexual feeling of any kind, and in this was believed by so many, had clearly never come across women like Sovrina, nor my dalliance of the previous evening, or the host of other women who had from time to time come to the Cock and Hen Club that Cockburn and I had run in Brighton, or The Nunnery in Rusper. The ladies came not for money, of course, but were driven by boredom and lust. Indeed, they could sometimes be persuaded to offer me loans to overcome my more pressing financial problems. . . .

Believe me. I was thinking of such philosophical matters as I stared at the sky and contemplated mentally my recent excited couplings; I had no idea what was running through Cockburn's mind, of course, until abruptly he brought me back to our reason for being on *The Zouave*. 'This Charles Newton: his evidence will be crucial. But you say you have thoughts about it. . . ?'

I hesitated, brought back to the present from my dreaming. I realized it was time to bring Cockburn back to reality, also. 'Yes. Newton. The defence might be able to show he is lying; they may prove it wasn't *possible* for him to have sold the poison to Palmer.'

Cockburn frowned, scratched uneasily at his receding thatch of red hair. Somewhat irritably, he said, 'What are you driving at, James?'

'It's a problem with the provable *facts*,' I said.

'Isn't it always? What particular facts are you referring to?'

'Newton. The *timing* of the sale of strychnia.'

'What about it? Newton's evidence—'

'Can be controverted.'

Cockburn stared at me, his brow thunderous. 'We've gone over the whole prosecution case. All right, I concede we'll have difficulty with Professor Taylor's testimony and—'

'Newton is prepared to swear that on the night Cook died Palmer came to Dr Salt's premises and bought three grains of strychnia. He will place the timing of the sale as nine o'clock on the evening that John Parsons Cook died.'

'That is so. Where's the problem?'

'Ben Gully has done a deal of checking for me. We know that Palmer had gone to London on business that day and returned to Stafford that evening, by train. Ben has checked train times. The London train reaches Stafford at 8.45 p.m. From there Palmer would have had to travel to Rugeley by fly: transport is normally obtained at the Talbot Arms. Even if he managed to get a fly immediately he could not have got to Rugeley *before ten minutes after ten.*'

Cockburn was silent, staring moodily into his glass of brandy-and-water. 'Who can prove this?'

'The man employed at the Talbot Arms to convey passengers is one Allspice. Gully's talked to him. He avers he did indeed pick up Palmer from the London train. And conveyed him to Rugeley. Arriving after ten at night.'

Cockburn gritted his teeth. 'Have the defence spoken to Allspice yet?'

'Probably. But that's not all. It won't be down only to Allspice. If the defence call him they will probably also call one Jeremiah Smith to corroborate the time of arrival.'

'Then maybe Newton was mistaken about the time of sale of the strychnia,' Cockburn muttered irritably. 'We'll have to get him to change his story. This man Jeremiah Smith—'

'He claims he met Palmer off the fly at Rugeley when Allspice delivered him and then took him directly to see Palmer's mother. So there was no sale of strychnia by Newton. And even if there was, Palmer could not have had time to prepare the pills—containing the poison—to administer them to Cook. The timings are all against us.'

Cockburn glowered, bringing his rufus eyebrows together in a frown. 'Your man Gully has dug a deep hole for us.'

I waved my brandy glass airily. 'Then there's the argument that Palmer needed the strychnia to poison Cook, to escape his financial obligations. Well, I have a man on the ground in Rugeley—'

'Ben Gully again, I imagine,' Cockburn remarked with a slight smile.

I nodded. 'He's found a man called Harry Cockayne, who looks after Palmer's horses. Cockayne will give evidence that he intended shooting some dogs which had been harassing Palmer's horses. He will say that Palmer suggested that strychnia could be used to poison the hounds in question, rather than using a gun.'

Cockburn chewed at his upper lip. 'A use for the poison. . . .'

'Exactly. And a plausible one. And as for killing Cook for financial gain, there's Will Saunders, the trainer from Palmer's stables at Hednesford. At the Grand Jury in Stafford he has already deposed that Cook had sent for him shortly before he died, gave him some money to settle debts and told him he'd given all the rest to Palmer to settle urgent business affairs in London.'

Cockburn nodded, grimacing. 'Thus removing the financial motive for Cook's murder. I see what the defence will raise: Why kill Cook if no money was owing? We'll want to show there was money owed, that Palmer had stolen the money Cook won at Shrewsbury, but if Will Saunders is telling the truth that story won't hold up. But putting that to one side, if we can't prove that Palmer bought the strychnia, and had time to prepare the pills—'

'That's what Jeremiah Smith will state, that there *was* no time. He's an important witness. The defence will call him to prove that Palmer could *not* have bought strychnia from Newton at nine in the evening, and that the good doctor was with his mother when the poison was supposed to have been made up into pills.'

Cockburn frowned, squinted up at the winter sky. 'The mother, Sarah Palmer, will she stand by her son with this statement?'

'She believes her Billy a saintly person.'

Silence fell between us. Cockburn drained his glass, poured himself another measure, added some water from the decanter on the table between us and performed the same service for me. He sat there thinking for a little while and then cocked a wary eye in my direction. 'I know you, James. I can't believe you've gone to the trouble of identifying these holes in our prosecution case without coming up with some scheme to overcome the problems.'

I smiled and raised one shoulder in a modest gesture of acknowledgement. 'First of all we can attack Jeremiah Smith. It turns out he's not only a friend of Palmer, negotiating loans with the assurance companies as a front man, but he also performs rather more personal services for the mother. It seems he shares the bed, quite regularly, of the elderly widow. She might be twenty years his senior but apparently she is still enthusiastic and active between the sheets.'

Cockburn straightened in his seat, one arm leaning on the gunwale. 'He's her lover? So his evidence could be shown to be biased in favour of her son!' He grimaced, considered the matter. 'Even so, it won't be enough. If Sarah Palmer herself states that Billy Palmer was at her side when he was supposed to be making the pills to be administered to Cook—'

'I think she can be persuaded *not* to give that evidence.'

There was a surprised glint in Cockburn's foxy eyes. 'And how are we going to undertake that persuasion, exactly?'

I was unable to keep the satisfaction out of my tone.

'Ben Gully's discovered that Mrs Sarah Palmer has had lovers before Jeremiah Smith. Sarah Palmer, in spite of her age, is a lusty woman. Before Jeremiah Smith took up the position in her bed there were predecessors, notably a certain feckless Irishman by the name of Duffy. Like Smith, also twenty years her junior. She became infatuated with him; paid his debts; entertained him in the afternoons. They had a passionate affair.'

A light breeze had risen. Cockburn laid back his head, sniffed the salty air. But I guessed he was also sniffing salty opportunities.

'During the course of their entanglement—Duffy had a wife in Ireland, by the way—Sarah Palmer wrote some fairly explicit letters detailing just what she got up to with him. After a while Duffy went back to Ireland and the letters were found among his effects at the inn he lodged in at Rugeley: he'd skipped without paying his bills, you see, and the landlord intended holding Duffy's goods as security. That included the letters. But his wife, she read the letters and hit upon a plan for recovering some of the money owed by Duffy. She used them to provide entertainment for her clients: she charged men in the bar the price of a glass of grog to have a look at the racy adventures of the aforesaid Widow Palmer and Duffy. Ben Gully read them. They don't just raise the hair on the back of your neck, apparently.'

Cockburn's eyes were gleaming. 'I think I see where you're going with this, James.'

I explained that Ben Gully, on my instructions, had already passed the information to Captain Hatton, Chief of Staffordshire Constabulary. He was persuaded this could be a matter of maintenance of public order and decency and had confiscated the letters. They remained in his possession. 'So, if Sarah Palmer takes the stand and declares her son was with her when we say he was making up the pills and poisoning Cook, we will naturally be bound to question her veracity as a witness. Her conduct with Jeremiah Smith will be exposed—thus blackening his testimony as well as hers—and we can also cause the Duffy letters to be read out in court. Her credibility as a witness will collapse. Worse, the letters will destroy whatever reputation she presently retains as an elderly widow. Wealthy she might be, but she won't want her sexual behaviour held up to the delight of all in the courtroom. No, she won't take the stand.'

Cockburn nodded thoughtfully. 'That takes care of defence witnesses Jeremiah Smith and Mrs Sarah Palmer. But there's still the evidence of the fly driver, Allspice. From what you say, Allspice agrees he was waiting at the Junction Hotel at 8.45 that evening, met the London train and then drove Palmer to Rugeley on that critical Monday evening. Arriving not till after ten ... when our witness, Newton, states he served Palmer with the strychnia at nine that evening, in Rugeley. If so—'

'We would have to abandon the claim that Palmer was given the strychnia at 9 p.m. And he would not have had time to make up the pills before he administered them to Cook.'

Cockburn was silent for a little while. He finished his second brandy, reached for the bottle, poured himself another. His hand was shaking slightly. 'Once again, I suspect, James, that from your demeanour you have a solution to these problems.'

I took a deep pull on my cigar. I knew Cockburn well by then, but what I was going to suggest might offend his sense of professionalism and legal propriety. I blew out the smoke in a determined gust, turned to hold his glance. 'The horse cooper, Harry Cockayne, the trainer, Will Saunders, and the fly driver, Allspice, they can all damage us with their evidence, so I would recommend we should subpoena them all *to give evidence for the Crown.*'

I could see the astonishment in Cockburn's features. 'But they can destroy our case!' Then the doubt in his little eyes gradually cleared. '*Subpoena* them. . . .'

'To subpoena them doesn't mean we have to *call* them,' I asserted. 'And the defence *can't* call them if they are *our* witnesses. . . .'

'That would shut out their evidence,' Cockburn mused. His eyes lit up. 'So we lock out Sarah Palmer, shred Smith . . . and subpoena the others.' He looked up at a darkening sky and I knew he agreed with my strategy. And that's how it fell out at the trial.

Jeremiah Smith gave evidence but was laughed out of court when he struggled to preserve the reputation of the wealthy, 60-year-old widow he was sleeping with, and the jury disregarded his story about meeting Palmer from the London train. After subpoenas were issued to the other possible defence witnesses we played safe: we smuggled Cockayne out of Staffordshire and warned him to lie low if he knew what was good for him; we packed the trainer Saunders well out of reach of the defence lawyers; and as for Allspice, well, we got him removed from his position as driver at the Junction Hotel and provided employment for him with the rural constabulary, well out in the country.

You look at me in astonishment. Why did leading defence counsel Serjeant Shee—who had replaced my friend Serjeant Wilkins—not accuse us of sharp practice? There's no doubt he could have done, and would have wanted to. But he had to face realities—and the pressure of his own personal ambition. To attack the Attorney General for doubtful practices would have ruined Shee's reputation and you need to be aware that at that time he was aiming for and expecting a judgeship himself. So he had to swallow the bitter pill.

You have a look on your face that suggests you believe our conduct was somewhat . . . *unethical*? You don't seem to understand, my boy. It's all a matter of tactics and *planning*. You have to look ahead, guess what the other side will be up to and undertake what is best for your case. It's like a military campaign, the practice of the law. And believe me, tricks like that have been tried on me from time to time, and I had been forced to back away.

Anyway, it worked. Charles Newton, and his doubtful evidence, was not overthrown. In the jury's minds, Palmer bought the strychnia that night, at nine in the evening, made it up into pills, and administered a fatal dose to Cook at the Talbot Arms, at 10.30 that evening. Smith was laughed out of court and Sarah

Palmer stayed away to nurse her reputation. The other damaging witnesses never made an appearance.

As I've already intimated to you, it's all a game. And winner takes all. Even so, it wasn't an easy progress. Far from it. There was plenty of rough riding to do that week in Westminster Hall.

You can imagine the intense public interest that was aroused by the case: after all, I had managed to arrange for an Act of Parliament to be hurriedly passed to bring the hearing away from Stafford to London, and it was the first case in which murder by strychnine poisoning was charged. And of course, the law courts had always been regarded almost as places of entertainment, while the murderers themselves were objects of intense curiosity, even years after they had been choked off. I myself recall that when I was a boy of twelve or so, I went to Bartholomew Fair to see the preserved head of the murderer Corder, the man who killed Maria Marten in the Red Barn. The head was on display and attracted numerous fascinated admirers, I can tell you. You're probably aware that the Red Barn murder has been a popular standby on the stage in the penny gaffs for the last fifty years or more. And that day at Bartholomew Fair there was even to be seen a printed account of the murder, bound in Corder's own skin: the only case, I believe, of a man being hung, drawn and *quarto-ed*! Hah!

It was inevitable that the Palmer trial would be a similar sensation to the populace at large. The streets outside Westminster Hall were packed, there were struggles to get inside to the courtroom and many disappointed men and women were turned away at the door.

My old friend Charlie Wilkins had already vanished from the scene as counsel for Palmer: shortly before trial he pleaded illness and cried off. In fact it wasn't a case of illness at all, for like me he was in deep financial trouble, his duns were after him and he'd managed to flee by fishing smack to Dieppe only with considerable difficulty. Poor old Charlie. I never did see him again. Nor did his creditors ever get their hands on him: he died in a foreign country, not long after. Which was why Palmer's defence was led by Serjeant Shee, QC, MP for Kilkenny. Problem was, he was an Irish Catholic and London juries continued to hold strong prejudices against Romanists. Advantage to us, again.

Palmer's defence faced another problem. The trial was to be handled by none other than Lord Chief Justice Campbell. Now I'd always got on well with Jack Campbell, in spite of his fearsome reputation. It think it harked back to my first appearance before him years earlier. He snarled at me in court once, when I was a junior barrister, ordering me to sit down. I remained standing. He glowered at me, admonished me again: 'I told you to sit down!' I held my ground, not wishing to be dominated in such a way. He ended by roaring at me 'Mr James, I tell you for the last time to *sit down!*'

I stared at him coolly, and replied, 'I'm sorry, my lord. I didn't realize you were addressing me. I thought you were speaking to the usher!'

He glared at me in fury for a few seconds and then his mouth twitched, he leaned back and he said no more. The fact is, Jack Campbell used to like barristers who were prepared to stand up to him from time to time, and he also enjoyed my ready wit. The judge and I, we often bandied jokes at each other in the following years.

But Jack Campbell was a man of the manse, a Scot like the Attorney General, and I knew he was going to be on our side. Beside him on the bench that week was my old adversary Baron Alderson—he had no love for me nor Cockburn, but his hatred of the Turf biased him against Palmer and his love of nags. I dare say there was only Mr Justice Cresswell as the third judge who was prepared to play fair, but he was always a timid fellow, and easily browbeaten by stronger personalities.

And indeed, that was how it went.

Take the medical witnesses. Lord Chief Justice Campbell allowed the seven prosecution witnesses to take seats, and eulogized them to the jury; but he made the defence medical witnesses stand in the aisles for hours until called. Then he constantly sneered at the evidence they gave in the witness box. Baron Alderson also made his own feelings regularly felt, by twisting his face, muttering 'Humbug!' at some defence evidence and waving his hands expressively at the jury whenever a witness displeased him. And when I was on my feet, Jack Campbell allowed me a deal of licence in the asking of illegitimate questions: as I've said before now, he was always partial to me, the old rogue.

As for us, Cockburn took our witnesses through the case, showing that though a friend of Cook, Palmer had in fact been robbing him, owed him money and finally got rid of him by administering poison in the form of strychnia. The fact that the defence experts swore to natural causes led to such conflicting medical evidence that we were able to tie up the jury in mental knots: the conflict in detail was made the most of, leaving the jury stunned with incomprehension as witnesses contradicted each other, and themselves. We had schooled the maid who had taken some broth to Cook during his illness to insinuate it had been prepared by Palmer. We got her to say she had sipped it, and had been taken ill. We skated successfully over the fact that she had never given such evidence earlier at the inquest.

We managed to persuade another maid to speak of twitching and convulsions during the death throes as evidence of strychnine poisoning, even though, once again, she had omitted to give such evidence at the inquest. And after Charles Newton gave his crucial evidence I took him back to the previous November when he had gone to Palmer's house in the evening.

'What did he say to you?' I asked.

'He asked me what dose of strychnia would be required to kill a dog. I told him, a grain. He then asked me whether it would be found in the stomach after death.'

'What did you say?'

'I told him there would be no inflammation and that I did not think it would be found.'

'What did he remark upon that?'

'I think he said: "It's all right!" as if speaking to himself. Then he did *that*.'

At this point the lying rogue snapped his fingers and the courtroom roared in indignant anger. Neither the spectators, nor the jury, seemed to consider it odd that a qualified medical man like Dr Palmer should be asking such questions of an apothecary's unqualified assistant.

And Harry Cockayne wasn't there to assert that Palmer might have wanted the drug for the purpose mentioned: to kill dogs harassing his mares at Hednesford. Saunders didn't appear to assert that Palmer didn't need Cook's money; and the fly driver, Allspice, well, he was comfortably ensconced as an officer in the rural constabulary—and unavailable for the trial.

Cockburn made an eight hour speech on the last of the twelve days. I'd written most of it for him, of course. It was later described as masterly. But it was the Lord Chief Justice who really did for Palmer in the end, and the fraudulent doctor knew it. Jack Campbell summed up strongly for the prosecution and we got a verdict: Dr Palmer was found guilty of murdering his friend John Parsons Cook by administering strychnine pills to him—in spite of the medical fact that there was not a trace of the poison in his body.

Of course, there was a huge outcry in the newspapers over the next few weeks: the weaknesses of the prosecution case were pointed out; demands were made to discover why certain witnesses were missing; the College of Surgeons was in uproar and Professor Taylor excoriated by his colleagues; there were strictures upon Campbell's handling of the case. I came under fire for asking questions that should have been overruled by the Lord Chief Justice as illegal and irrelevant, but Jack Campbell had let me carry on, which I did cheerfully, bringing in all the local Staffordshire prejudicial gossip—obtained from Ben Gully—that was available to me.

I mean, if you are given licence by the bench, you have to make the fullest use of it.

But these omissions and tergiversations, while pointed out by defence counsel, none of it did the doctor any good.

He was hanged at Stafford Gaol, still cool as you might wish. He gave no dying declaration from the scaffold. He never confessed. The crowd was disappointed. All he was later reported as saying to the hangman was, when standing over the trapdoor, he asked 'Is it safe?'

Cool to the end.

And looking back, did I believe justice was done? Let me put it like this. Billy Palmer was a rogue and a cheat, a forger and a swindler, but I don't believe for a moment that he was a murderer. Not of Cook, anyway. As for the rest of the claims, well, he was never tried for the other alleged murders, and a lot of it was just gossip anyway.

Still, it was another *cause célèbre* to add to my growing reputation. A week later I called in at the Reform Club. In the smoking room I came across Cockburn: he was drinking a glass of claret with Sir James Duke and Viscount Palmerston. Old Pam smiled when he saw me enter, called me over. Congratulated me on the support I'd given the Attorney General.

Then he wrinkled his nose, and shook his head. 'You know, the Home Secretary, Sir George Grey has had to deal with a great deal of pressure from the Press. The defence counsel, they have made much of the discrepancy in the medical evidence, the missing witnesses, the character of that Newton fellow, and Lord Chief Justice Campbell's summing up and direction to the jury. But we have to stand by the verdict—and the man was a rogue, wasn't he?'

'Undoubtedly,' Cockburn and I chorused.

'Anyway, the Home Secretary is standing by Campbell. Dammit, we can't undermine the Lord Chief Justice!' He scowled. 'And there's the matter of the assurance companies, in addition.'

'The companies?' I asked, surprised.

The Prime Minister smiled wryly. 'They paid out a deal of money to support the prosecution case: if Palmer hadn't hanged they'd have had to pay out on several policies that would have fallen due!'

'And there's the matter of a directorship in one of the companies, for Sir George Grey,' Sir James Duke murmured, giving me a wink.

Palmerston harrumphed. 'We'll not talk about that possibility, gentlemen. Fact is, Grey refused as Home Secretary to exercise the prerogative of mercy. Still, we were wise bringing the case down to Westminster Hall. The London juries can be relied upon to bring in the right verdict.' He ran a hand over his bald head and sighed. 'Meanwhile, there's been a lot of talk in Rugeley Town Hall, about the infamous reputation the place now has because of Palmer's misdeeds. I'm expecting a delegation from the Mayor of Rugeley tomorrow. They want me to arrange an Act of Parliament: they want to change the name of the town and wipe out the Palmer connection from men's minds.'

I glanced at Cockburn, then, in an offhand manner, I said, 'You could satisfy their desire, I'm sure, Prime Minister.'

'How?' he asked irritably.

'Tell them you'll arrange a change of name by all means . . . provided they name the town after you.'

For a moment he seemed nonplussed, and then a delighted smile crossed his baby-like features. *'Palmerstown!'* he cried.

And that's what he did, apparently, when they called to see him. They were well out of the room, however, before they realized what a joke had been played on them. And they didn't take up the suggestion he made to them, so the town is called Rugeley to this day, notorious as the home base of the infamous murderer, Dr William Palmer.

A few nights later, seeking recreation, I found myself at the gaming tables at Crockford's. I was losing, as usual and was on the point of calling it a night when I became aware of someone standing at my elbow at the chicken hazard table.

I stared at him. 'What the damnation are *you* doing here?'

Inspector Redwood was dressed appropriately for an evening out on the town: smart frock coat, yellow waistcoat, polished boots, a bunch of fresh violets in his buttonhole. He smiled, unabashed. 'Like you, sir, I seek relaxation, a little entertainment. Which fortunately I am able to do, while still acting in a detective capacity.' Seeing my lack of understanding, he glanced around and then leaned towards me confidentially. 'I am here to keep an eye on a certain person of quality—I am unable to inform you of the reason. But you must be aware that we of the Detective Force are often employed privately to assist in investigations outside our normal occupations. Inspector Whicher, for instance, is much involved in the Kent family's investigation of the mysterious affair at Road— he avers it is his conviction that the killing was done by Miss Constance Kent. And then you will have come across the work of my colleague Inspector Field, seeking the perpetrators of the Great Bullion Robbery. He was for a while involved in the matter you have recently pursued—the murderous William Palmer.'

He paused, eyed me for several seconds and then continued in a somewhat lower tone. 'For myself, I remain . . . fascinated by the death of Lord George Bentinck.'

The familiar cold hand touched my heart. 'That matter has been long put to rest. He died of natural causes.'

Redwood smiled cynically. 'That's what the Palmer defence counsel asserted was how John Parsons Cook died.'

'The cases are not comparable!' I snapped.

'Indeed not,' Redwood agreed complaisantly. 'But the matter still churns over in my mind. And for me, your work for the prosecution of Palmer stirred matters even further. You seem to know a great deal about poisons, Mr James. Particularly those which leave no traces in the body thereafter.'

I took a deep breath. 'That's nonsense!'

'Perhaps so, but I wonder if that is how Lord George met his end?' He paused, watching me carefully. 'And you know, oddly enough, there has come to my ears recently a rumour that on the day his lordship died near Welbeck Abbey, you were seen in the vicinity ....'

A roar came up from a neighbouring table as the winner celebrated a success at *rouge et noir*, a position I rarely reached. Redwood glanced around, caught sight of his quarry for the night heading for the doors and excused himself quickly. 'I fear I must leave. But perhaps we might speak again at some time, Mr James, about the fate of Lord George Bentinck. When I have more time—and perhaps more information—at my disposal ....'

He disappeared through the throng. I remained for a while, but was left with a sick feeling in my stomach, and no appetite for further adventures at the gaming table that night.

The spectre of Lord George still seemed to hover over me and I wondered whether that wisp of malice would ever be laid to rest.

PART FOUR

1

Success for Cockburn and for me in the Palmer trial soon produced their rewards. Cockburn was appointed Recorder of Bristol and my name was put forward for the position of Recorder of Brighton. The Jervis promises had been fulfilled, and I was in the limelight as, effectively, a junior judge, gaining experience before a full judgeship could be awarded me. But while Cockburn slid easily and without criticism into his seat at Bristol—it was his second such appointment—for me there were still echoes of Horsham resounding in Whitehall.

As soon as my appointment to Brighton was announced a stir was made in the House of Commons by a Tory nonentity called Craufurd. He was a member of my Inn, a follower of the deceased Lord George Bentinck, a committed mud-thrower and out to blacken my name in consequence. There was the additional motive, of course: he had hoped to obtain the post of Recorder of Brighton for himself.

It need hardly be said that his petition for my removal was notably unpopular with the Government, where my standing was high. Sir John Jervis had been involved at Horsham alongside me, as had Sir Alexander Cockburn; Craufurd attacked them in his speech and furthermore, Viscount Palmerston was by implication involved in that Craufurd claimed he had shown favouritism by recommending me, a fellow member of the Reform Club, to the Brighton position. The consequence was that the political ranks closed quickly behind me, in support.

Craufurd's words were intemperate and ill-chosen: he referred to the Horsham campaign, and drew attention to my rejection by the benchers of the Inner Temple, before unwisely suggesting that a *'connection with the Government was clearly the finest guarantee of judicial office'*—an indirect and offensive allusion to Lord Palmerston. Pompously, Craufurd announced that the Recordership was an appointment of a judicial character *'the holder of which should be above the slightest breath of suspicion'*. Effectively, he was stating that my character was not of that kind.

Now I have to admit that in a certain light he was not far wrong, but his performance exposed him to Cockburn's blistering reply. Cockburn, as sitting Member for Southampton, derided Craufurd for want of taste, attacks on a judge—Sir John Jervis—who could not defend himself in the House, prejudicial comments against me, which had been raised only when Craufurd had failed in his own candidature for Brighton, and the 'stale' story of Horsham. He summed up Craufurd's insinuations as a personal, envious attack upon the man who had been appointed to the Brighton position: me. Craufurd's lamentable reply was wild and so badly directed that he lost even the support of his own party. The motion to inquire into my conduct was lost and the House even decided to expunge the matter from the Journals of the House, to teach the lesson that proceedings were not to be used as the vehicle for imputations on private character.

So I had triumphed and when I took up my position *The Brighton Herald* announced itself to be impressed by *'an able lawyer who showed an ability that bore comparison with any of the higher courts'*.

But Craufurd taught me a lesson. The death of Bentinck did not mean I lacked enemies. My friends and supporters warned me to take more care, and proceed with more discretion, but an innate stubbornness on my part meant that I saw no reason to change my performances in court or the somewhat rackety progress—I freely admit this—of my personal life.

For I reasoned I was not alone: in a new fog of moral panic at the Bar I was being singled out for personal attacks, criticism of behaviour that was not uncommon in political, literary or even the highest social circles. You should appreciate, my boy, in spite of the prejudices which Prince Albert had instilled in the Queen since their marriage, which led to constitutional crises from time to time, scandals *abounded*: we were all at it. Apart from the Prime Minister, still a skirt-chaser in spite of his advancing age, there was the example set by Lord Wilton, taking the arrogant step of actually introducing his companion—a noted whore called Caroline Cook—to the Queen herself. Wilton had taken a house in Cleveland Gardens for Miss Cook, had introduced her to the officers' mess at Woolwich and had had the temerity to introduce her, as 'Miss Beales', to the Queen at the Hanover Ball. Then there was my friend, Cockburn. I've already mentioned his reputation as a womanizer, and spoken of the children he fathered on a butcher's wife, but he also spawned a daughter and two sons on a certain Louise Godfrey—whom he never married, and lived with quite openly. There was Charlie Dickens: he cast aside his wife of thirty years to take up with the young actress Ellen Ternan. There was Thackeray who had picked up an infectious disease in Belgium brothels before placing his wife in an asylum and spending the next twenty years impotently lusting after a friend's wife, Jane Brookfield. There was Wilkie Collins, not only having two mistresses at the same time but actually co-habiting with them at establishments within walking distance of each other! And don't forget the poets—Swinburne, of course, was notorious for his addiction to being caned by middle-aged women, preferably as he emerged naked from the sea, and even in the States there was Walt Whitman, who enjoyed young boys . . . . I often wonder, what *is* it about poets? And we won't even get started on the Agapemone cult—which involved public fornication with the religious leader on an altar—or what else clergymen got up to in their spare time!

I have to admit there were rumours enough about me. Some of them were true. Shortly after I took up the Recordership of Brighton I had to beg off court appearances for a short period while recovering from a second bout of the clap, acquired after some drunken celebrations at The Nunnery with a certain actress I had earlier represented in court: it was discreetly reported in the newspapers that I was suffering from an abscess of the thigh. But let's be clear: neither that, nor my activities of the Cock and Hen variety seemed to deter members of the fair sex—including the lady I told you about, whose bedroom I had failed to attain on that eventful occasion at the Earl of Yarborough's house.

Incidentally, that lady—Marianne Hilliard—came to see me when I was still confined mainly to my bed at The Nunnery with my painful condition.

She explained she continued to live in Paris and Boulogne but had returned to England briefly to attend the reading of her late husband's will. For it seemed that the obnoxious Crosier Hilliard had suddenly passed away. His life of libidinous licentiousness, cockfighting, pugilism, rowdyism and whoring had finally concluded at Fareham after eight days confined to his bed.

'Eight days of delirium tremens,' Marianne calmly explained to me as she sat in my parlour, dressed in conventional widow weeds even though she clearly cared nothing for the man who had been her husband. 'And his estate amounted to virtually nothing after his wild expenditures. A horse, a dog, a sword and two portraits of himself. Little more.'

'But you,' I asked. 'You are comfortably placed?'

She inclined her head gracefully. 'I was given nothing in his will, but I am well provided for, fortunately, and happy in my life in France. The social ostracism consequent upon familial separation does not extend to the salons there. The fortune left me by my father was always secure from my husband's predations. My daughter is with me for company, so life is quiet, but acceptable.'

I had in fact heard some vague rumours about her behaviour in Boulogne, involving a military man from her husband's own regiment, so I concluded her life was not all *that* quiet. And on this occasion, as she looked at me I caught a glimpse of coquetry: our glances seemed to merge, to become locked, to become inextricably entangled and I felt a return of the stirring emotion which had moved me on the night Viscount Palmerston had blundered between us in the darkened corridor at Lord Yarborough's residence. But as I rearranged myself in my chair and felt a spasm of pain between my thighs I forced myself to look away: in view of the present condition of my masculine appurtenances I did not feel that I could make the appropriate advances to deepen our relationship. Pretty speeches are unwise when you're suffering from the clap.

So the moment passed again, a week later she returned to Boulogne and we did not see each other for a number of years.

But my professional career was reaching an entirely new level. I had become not only a social, but a legal lion. In view of the skills I had already demonstrated I was called upon to act as an election agent again, working for Captain David Pelham, the brother of the Earl of Yarborough. *The Boston Advertiser* reported cockades, brass bands, railway navigators smashing windows and a pitched battle in the streets: inevitably, Pelham's opponent complained of shameful intimidation and bribery. Nevertheless, I steered Pelham home to a seat in the Commons and the Earl showed his gratitude thereafter by numerous invitations to his home. And his impressionable 14-year-old son, Lord Worsley, became even more dog-like in his devotion: he demonstrated what can only be described as an infatuation for me and my deeds. This led to my introducing him to some of the more elegant night houses and, I admit, calling upon him from time to time to endorse bills which were falling due at inconvenient, financially embarrassing times for me. But what should a man do, if not call on his friends when in trouble?

And trouble, in financial matters, there still was. Even though a cascade of briefs poured into my chambers and my earnings steadily rose until I was soon to become the highest-paid barrister in England—really, my boy, it's true—I was still crippled by debt, paying as much as one hundred and eighty per cent to some of my creditors to avoid being dunned. I was constantly forced to take loans at exorbitant rates merely to pay interest of previous debts. The society in which I moved demanded expenditure at an alarming scale; the socially great sought my presence at their soirées; Sir James Duke and the Duke of Norfolk, Lord Pelham, Lord Combermere and Lord Wilton, the Earl of Yarborough and Viscount Palmerston—they all demanded my presence at their country houses and a procession of society ladies fluttered breathily into my arms—often paying for the pleasure later by way of loans of considerable size.

A social and legal lion. . . . It was a time when most of the 'flash' cases came my way at nisi prius: *The Daily News* briefed me in the libel suit brought by Lord Lucan, who was complaining of their criticisms of his conduct in the Crimean campaign: in the witness box I cut him to ribbons, deriding him and Lord Cardigan as being like two great schoolgirls in their private feuding which led to the disaster of the charge of the Light Brigade. I made the forgetful Lord Combermere, ancient hero of the Peninsular War, look the doddering fool he was—though he still cheerily invited me to his home where his wife refused to speak to me—and my table in chambers was littered with crim.con briefs.

But my aspirations towards a seat in Parliament seemed to have stalled; I was becalmed, as a man of your background might say. I still wanted—*needed*—to attain my political prizes, and they still seemed far distant . . . until I thought the opportunity had finally arisen at Southampton.

The vacancy caused by the sudden asthmatic death of Sir John Jervis, who had been elevated to the bench after the Horsham by-election, left a judicial seat open and Cockburn was the obvious choice to become Chief Justice of the Common Pleas. As a judge, he would have to relinquish his seat at Southampton, and I had the support of Palmerston and the Radical party.

But Cockburn dithered.

'I'm reluctant to give up my present life, James,' he confided to me, as he sipped at his brandy and water. 'My large professional income will obviously drop if I take a seat on the Bench, the hurly-burly of political life will be lost to me and, well, to put not too fine a point on it, the pleasurable diversions which you and I have enjoyed together at The Nunnery will have to come to an end.'

Then, while he was still chewing things over in his mind, a by-election was called for Hull. Rather than wait upon Cockburn's decision, I decided to throw my cap into that particular ring. After committing myself to a considerable degree of expenditure in that estimable town I then heard that Cockburn had decided to accept the Common Pleas after all. And at a subsequent meeting in the Reform Club I was persuaded by him and Palmerston and Sir James Duke that Southampton was a better bet than Hull, and that the voters there would welcome me with open arms.

So, as was reported in *The Hampshire Advertiser*, '*Down came Mr James, duly labelled QC, endorsed with the crabbed and unmistakeably legal hand of Sir Alexander Cockburn.*'

Unfortunately, my friends had not advised me well; it seemed Southampton had had enough of lawyers representing them. I well recall the campaign that was rolled out against me: I found myself in the middle of a battle at Pratt's Riding School where a continuous chanting of *No lawyers, No lawyers* drowned out my election address. At the point where the platform on which I stood was overturned I beat a hasty retreat and although I manfully promised my supporters next day at the Royal Hotel that I would not be deterred and would continue the fight, on my return to London discretion—and financial embarrassment—prevailed and I decided otherwise. I had at that time taken a town house in Bedford Place. I told my supporters who gathered there that I was withdrawing from the bruising battle for the Southampton seat.

Unreasonably, Cockburn was somewhat sniffy with me for a while thereafter, and the Prime Minister himself was a little put out of countenance but in reality I had little choice: my financial situation was becoming alarming. I had spent freely at Hull and now again at Southampton and there was the likelihood of a general election the following year. I could not afford to buy a seat I might hold only for a short period. I needed to stiffen my financial sinews and await the best opportunity.

And that would mean I needed briefs in the election committees which would inevitably follow the appointing of a new House of Commons. I concluded that to seek a seat myself at that time was something beyond my financial capabilities.

So after the Southampton debacle I set aside political ambitions for a while and worked myself into a professional frenzy. I took everything I could: I found myself representing dog fanciers and jockeys, a mayor who failed to pay his wine bill in a brothel and a mourning relative who complained that the funeral coach had overturned on the way to the cemetery, leaving the dear departed lying in the road. We achieved substantial damages for the affront: natural in a Christian community! I attacked reputations and humbug, exposed scandals and hypocrisy, railed against aristocrats, brewery owners and politicians and attained columns of notices in the national press. Not that it was all court work: I needed to enlarge my social contacts. Christmas came and I took out a game licence and did some shooting at the Duke of Norfolk's estates, at the Duke's personal invitation; I was seen at Friday to

Mondays in Hampshire, Kent and Nottingham and I fished in the Thames, the Ouse and the Wear. Then it was back to work. I sat as Recorder in Brighton, dealt with hearings for breach of promise and nuisance and I rode the circuit with success. Consequently, by the spring of the following year, when election fever was at its height, I was £4,000 richer . . . in theory, at least.

And after I attended Sir Richard Bethell's big dinner at the Albion Tavern in Aldersgate Street, when the results of the general election were in the frenzied avalanche of work began again; retainers for the election committee hearings flooded into my chambers and I found myself scurrying between committee rooms, with the consequence that my name was being heard and noted in every county in England and not a few in Ireland, also.

I found my personal popularity with the political party of my choice rose also, not least because of the spat I had with Gladstone. I spoke in court, during *Lyle v Herbert*, a crim.con. case, of a former minister of the Crown who had once acted like a common detective, tracking the wife of a noble Duke through Italy, before becoming a witness to her frailty in the subsequent hearing for her adultery with Lord Lincoln.

Ha, yes, you remind me, I've already mentioned that particular episode to you. But did I tell you about the device used by the private enquiry agent? You see, when the grocer I was representing began to suspect his wife of infidelity he employed a detective who obtained proof of guilt with his patent crimconometer. The detective bored a hole in the bedroom wall and ran a string to it, tied to the bedsprings. The other end of the cord was attached to his device in the other room, which looked like a kind of thermometer, with a pointer which oscillated, recording the activity – and number of persons – in the bed beyond the wall. The grocer and his private enquiry agent waited, with cigars and porter, watching the crimconometer do its work and when the determined activity in the bedroom was at its height they rushed in and surprised the guilty couple, causing the adulterer to fall out of bed. They removed his boots so he couldn't escape and went back into the other room to discuss the whole affair.

When the case came on the other side sneered about the 'dirty activities' of the enquiry agent: I responded by comparing it to Gladstone's hunting down of the Duke of Newcastle's wife when she ran off to Italy with Lord Lincoln. Gladstone's furious reaction next day to what he considered as a slur – comparing him to a low-born private investigator – delighted Old Pam and the Liberal Party, as did the flurry of letters between Gladstone and myself: I had tweaked Gladstone's nose, I was their darling, the social lion who had shown his legal teeth.

They talked to me, they flattered me, these political luminaries. They insisted I was needed in the House with my wit, my capacity for cutting satire, and my eloquence and political conviction. We all waited for the first by-election to come about, where I could follow my star.

But while I waited, an immensely important brief fell into my legal lap. It was just what my reputation needed; a sensational hearing with political overtones, a case which would elevate me to the position of perhaps the most well known advocate in England.

It all began with an explosion in the crowded Rue de Pelletier in Paris, at the corner of the grand boulevards crowded with people to welcome the appearance of Napoleon III and Empress Eugénie. They were on their way to the opera, to attend the benefit performance of the renowned baritone Massini. They were about to descend from the imperial Berlin coach when there was a thunderous roar and all hell seemed to fall in upon them.

2

The procession had formed up in the Tuileries, the imperial coach escorted by a troop of Lancers, resplendent in their blue and white uniforms, along with the Imperial Guard under the leadership of the Commandant of Paris.

Dressed immaculately in black the Emperor sat beside Eugénie, in evening dress under a white cashmere cloak. With them was General Roquet, a hero of Waterloo. They were a little late arriving at the theatre but as the Lancers wheeled into review order the coachman reined in the horses to enter the carriageway where awaited the Master of Ceremonies and the Duke of Saxe-Coburg. Yes, that's right, the same family as our own coxcomb Prince Albert. As the party was about to descend from the carriage, in the crowd Felice Orsini gave the signal and Antonio Gomez threw the first bomb.

The grenade landed among the Lancers and burst like a cannon, causing widespread destruction. The heavy glass candelabra above the entrance to the Opera crashed down in a thousand deadly fragments and almost immediately the second bomb was thrown, launched by the second assassin, Carlo Rudio. It killed the Emperor's coachman and one of the horses; all the gas lamps in the street went out as shrieks of pain and cries of terror mingled with the clattering of wild hoofs and the shrill, terrified whinnying of frightened and injured horses.

As the Lancers clattered forward to shield the coach, the third bomb was thrown, this time by Orsini himself. It killed the other carriage horse and started a scurrying stampede of fugitives down the panicked boulevards.

All was confusion: Lancers, pedestrians, gendarmes, footmen and wild-eyed stallions dashed about in noisy confusion. A fourth grenade might have ended everything, but it never came.

The attempt on the life of the Emperor had failed. Napoleon III and his Empress emerged shakily from the ruined carriage and picked their way through the carnage into the Opera House. The first act of *William Tell* was over when they entered. News of the bombs swept through the theatre and the audience rose, cheered Emperor and Empress and the orchestra struck up triumphantly with the Bonapartist anthem *Partant pour la Syrie.*

Himself wounded, after throwing his bomb, Orsini had stumbled into Rue Lafitte, leaving a trail of blood; Gomez had taken refuge in the Ristorante Broggi; Rudio had concealed himself in a local tavern. But why had the fourth bomb not been thrown? The reason was that the fourth terrorist Guiseppe Pieri had been arrested before the first grenade had been launched and foolishly, in custody when he heard the first explosion, had cried out 'Do what you want with me! The first blow is struck!'

Gomez was quickly arrested as was Rudio; before daybreak the *Surêté* found Orsini asleep on his blood-soaked pillow.

Next morning, at the Café Suisse in London a little Belgian doctor called Simon Bernard was told of the events in Paris.

As you might imagine, my boy, the attempt upon the life of the Emperor enraged the French Government and sent a shudder throughout Europe, for it was the first time a bomb had been used in an attempted assassination, and the slaughter of innocent victims—eight dead and one hundred and fifty injured—was horrific. Very quickly, England's reputation as a sanctuary for political exiles came under attack: the French Press, and *Le Moniteur* in particular described London as the 'haunt of assassins' and England as the 'laboratory of murder'.

Palmerston bowed to French pressure and brought in a bill, the Conspiracy to Murder Act, which would give the Government power to treat plots hatched in England against foreign princes as felonies, triable in English courts. He failed to gauge the mood of the House; he was defeated, and immediately resigned. For, aided by French detectives the London police had discovered that the plan to assassinate Napoleon III had been hatched in London.

And the prime mover had been Dr Simon Bernard.

Orsini, Gomez, Rudio and Pieri had been the bomb throwers but Bernard had been the conspirator who preached revolution in France, Belgium and England; it was he who had persuaded Orsini that the assassination of the Emperor was a political necessity; it was Bernard who had helped manufacture the bombs in Birmingham, helped recruit the assassins, paid the conspirators, procured passports for them and acted as the go-between in London, Birmingham and Paris. He was arrested and charged before the magistrates at Bow Street. Meanwhile, Sir Fitzroy Kelly—old Applepip himself—had succeeded Cockburn as Attorney General and consulted several leading counsel as to whether a charge of murder would stick against Dr Bernard in an English court. I was one of those consulted.

I told Fitzroy Kelly I thought it *could* be done but by the time he approached me again I had done some hard thinking, and reached other conclusions.

I was always a gambling man—in the courts as well as the night houses. I could see significant possibilities in the Bernard case. And in those few days since the Attorney General first raised the matter with me I had evidence of the standing in which I was now held at the English Bar. As in the Palmer criminal trial, I was approached by both prosecution and defence. In addition, I had become aware of the political implications of the case. There was a platform of defiance that I could stand on—and *rage*.

Accordingly, when John Greenwood, Solicitor to the Treasury wrote to me offering me the brief for the prosecution I told him I had made my choice: defence attorneys had approached me and I had accepted their instructions. I would be acting for Dr Simon Bernard. For I realized that the brief, and the timing of the case, was of the utmost importance to me in my career.

You see, my boy, I've already told you that cross-examination is a peculiar skill but very alike to duel with the epée. One must attack aggressively, and defend stoutly, but it is also about badgering, deflecting, sniping, confusing, misleading, pricking, wounding, discountenancing and, finally, defeating. I was an acknowledged master of this skill. But there was another attribute for which I had become famous: the address to the jury.

I was known to be a *capital* man to a jury. My early training as a youth had been in the theatre, as I have mentioned. One needs a sense of theatre when one faces a jury. And aware as I was of the feeling which was sweeping the country, the heat engendered in comments made before the magistrates, the uproar in the Commons when Palmerston tried to bring in a bill which the public believed was a mere pandering to the French, I knew that I was being presented with an outstanding opportunity.

As soon as I received instructions from the defence attorneys I visited Bernard at his ghastly accommodation in Newgate.

It was a gloomy location for a gloomy discussion. The facts were before me, incontrovertible, and as I talked with Bernard I did not prevaricate: I informed him that his position, legally, was a hopeless one. The only cheerful thing about the whole thing was Dr Bernard himself: he was a dark-haired man, aquiline-nosed, but his cheery demeanour was almost amusing. I've met some cool characters in my time—Billy Palmer was one of the leaders in that respect—but Simon Bernard was the most cold-blooded individual I had ever came across. There was no doubt that he had conspired with Orsini: the grenades had been bought by Orsini but it was Bernard who had manufactured them in Birmingham, who had arranged for their transport to France and who had given the conspirators constant support. His involvement in the assassination plot had been deep and his guilt obvious. Indeed, he freely admitted his involvement. For he believed he was fighting for a Great Cause.

And he was not one of those dark, bearded, mysterious beings you read about in the penny dreadfuls hawked around the streets. He gave the lie to the stage impersonator of a conspirator. When I talked with him in that damp-walled gloomy cell his countenance was clear and cheerful, his conversation as free as though we were merely discussing the chances of the favourite winning the Derby. He seemed totally unconcerned with the danger of his situation, the peril of his position—more, it was as though he regarded himself as a hero of the first order.

It was this that gave me the first inkling of an idea for the manner in which I would conduct his defence.

I tried to impress upon him that a sentence of death from Lord Chief Justice Campbell was a racing certainty, if the jury found him guilty. Bernard seemed unmoved: he merely shrugged, raised his eyebrows and said, 'If I'm to be hanged, I must be hanged.'

But I knew we had a chance. The Crown prosecution had indicted him for murder but the Act under which he was charged spoke of deeds 'committed within the Queen's Peace'. The point was, Bernard's actions had caused deaths not in England, but in Paris, where the Queen's writ did not run. He was also charged with being an accessory to murder—but if the killing itself was not murder in England, how could he be regarded as an accessory to murder?

And in their rush to indict Bernard the Crown prosecutors had overlooked another problem. Neither Bernard nor Orsini were *subjects* of the Queen . . . so could proceedings properly lie against Simon Bernard, a foreigner, in English court of law?

These were nice points and I was determined to raise them, but more important in my view was the background to the hearing, the fragile relationship between the French and British Government and, not least of all, the general view held by the public. It was one of Francophobia. It was the view held by the rabble. And I knew I was perhaps the most effective rabble-rouser in the business, when it came to tapping into the public sentiment.

So my actions were planned carefully and deliberate in their aim.

When the trial opened at the Old Bailey it was among scenes reminiscent of the Palmer hearing, not least because I had taken the trouble to quietly leak to certain members of the press that this trial was not a simple one of murder, but a case involving the basic right of every Englishman to be free from the political pressure of foreign princes.

You liked that phrase, didn't you? I saw your eyes light up! They liked it in America too: President Lincoln himself mentioned it to me with approval when he welcomed me at a soirée at the White House in 1861.

So, when Dr Bernard stood in the dock in front of the Lord Chief Justice Campbell, flanked by the Lord Baron, Justice Erle and Justice Crowder, and my client pleaded not guilty I immediately rose, roaring my indignation, and attacked the court for want of jurisdiction. It was a forlorn hope, of course, and merely an opening salvo but I wanted to make the point and raise the heat at once. Campbell overruled me on the point, but conceded that Bernard would have the right to an English jury or one composed of his own countrymen.

I had schooled Bernard well.

In a clear, ringing tone he raised his chin and announced, 'I trust with confidence to a jury of Englishmen!'

This caused a stir of righteous pride in the packed courtroom, and brought the jury onto his side, as I had calculated. And I made a further point, with great deliberation.

'During the course of this hearing, my Lord, I shall be adverting to the unconscionable use by the prosecution of foreign spies. I must demand immediately that all such persons present in the courtroom shall be asked at once to withdraw!'

There was a moment's stunned silence, then, as twelve dark-clothed, black-bearded gentlemen stood up and made their way out of the courtroom a ripple of laughter went swirling among the crowded benches. The journalists loved it and scribbled mightily. I looked at Jack Campbell on the Bench and he caught my eye: there was the hint of a smile on his cruel lips, and I knew that he was well aware of what I was doing: the so-called spies were, of course, individuals I had arranged to be present, paid in advance, to undertake this manoeuvre.

But the jury, and the public did not know that.

I went on to hammer home the point about spies when I constantly referred to the use the Crown had made of the English police in liaising with their counterparts in France. I argued every single point in favour of my client, and threatened, when overruled, that I would take the matter to appeal. I needled the Attorney General, Sir Fitzroy Kelly, endlessly, both to irritate him and to raise the temperature of the proceedings. I drew sinister motives out of the collaboration between French and English authorities and intimated that there were truths behind this case that would never be disclosed (not that I really knew of any, of course). It was all flummery, you will appreciate, but the jury loved it; they were with me at every step, and brows were furrowed, eyes gleamed and pulses raced with indignation as their shoulders hunched in frustrated patriotism.

As each prosecution witness was paraded I not only emphasized their unreliability but also their foreign connections—some, I freely admit, imaginary—and stressed the political shenanigans which had been indulged in during the preparations for trial.

But it was when the Crown case was closed that I produced my trump card.

'My Lords, I will call no witnesses for the defence.'

There was a stunned silence in court; it extended to the judges on the bench, and then there was a slow gathering in the well of the packed courtroom of murmurs, puzzled chatter and amazed conversation. Their Lordships leaned towards each other, whispering. The society ladies seated beside them fluttered their fans in overheated excitement. Stays were strained, bosoms clutched.

Lord Chief Justice Campbell hammered on the table before him and fixed me with his eagle, withering, calculating eye.

'Do you mean to say, Mr James, that you will be content merely with addressing the jury?'

I bowed my bewigged head in confident assent. 'That is so, my Lord.'

Pandemonium broke out again but I continued to hold Jack Campbell's glance and detected the gleam in his eye: he knew what my game was to be.

And you know, in a way, when I rose to address the jury that day I was almost overwhelmed myself: I felt that it was almost as though I had been in training for this moment all my life. My whole career, not merely my professional training and experience, my knowledge of the common man, but also my early years treading the boards were to come together, strengthening my sinews for the contest I was about to make, the challenge I was about to throw down—the *performance* I was about to make.

Because this was to be theatre, pure, unadulterated theatre. The facts of the case, the evidence of the witnesses for the Crown, these matters were hardly relevant, and I had already decided that I would barely refer to them in my speech to the jury. I was to speak on higher things: the freedom of the individual, the corruption of Government and the rights of every free-born Englishman; I would argue Dr Simon Bernard was a principled man of the people struggling against the might of a French despot and a weak English Government; I would refer again to the doubtful legality of the proceedings in spite of Campbell's ruling and I would draw upon all I had learned in the stage training at John Cooper's academy those many years ago with its grand gestures and declamatory manner, the cut and thrust of argument in the lower courts and the tension and passion that I knew could be aroused in jurymen proud of their English heritage.

Rabble-rousing? Why deny it? Demagoguery? Of course! But that was the whole point—I was appealing to the jury's *emotions*, not the judge's view of the law!

Even now, after all the intervening years, I feel a rush of emotion about that day. A tear of pride prickles in my eye. The speech— ah, I tell you it was a notable triumph! After the event I had my speech published. I have a copy here—let me read you some of my perorations, and you will understand how I *worked* the jury.

'I should have thought that when, under the dim twilight of that morning, Orsini and Pieri expiated their crime upon the guillotine at Paris enough had been done to vindicate the demands of French justice! And when the English Government was defeated upon the Conspiracy Bill introduced to please the Emperor that the Crown prosecutors would have been satisfied! But no! They seek to find the prisoner guilty of the charge of murder under an Act of Parliament which is not applicable to this case! It is a mockery—and a sham!'

That put the cat among the pigeons, I can tell you! The infuriated shuffling among the Crown prosecutors, the brow-twitching grumbling and glaring on the Bench . . . but the jury was riveted.

I stood there, the sole champion of English freedoms in a corrupt court, my white-gloved left hand on my hip throwing back the skirt of my gown, my right hand extended as I had been taught on the stage, pointing, calling for the support of the gods, the ears of all who had gone before in the pursuit of liberty, my voice raised to a thunderous roar meant to be heard not just in the Old Bailey but in all the towns and cities and hamlets and rural by-lanes of the entire country. I rolled out the final words in triumphant, declamatory tones.

'Let the verdict be your own, uninfluenced by the ridiculous fears of French armaments, or French invasion. . . .'

Not that there had been any likelihood of such events, but that's beside the point.

'Tell the prosecutor in this case that the jury box is the sanctuary of English liberty!'

Stirring words, hey? And then there's this bit, a little later. Here we are:

'Tell the prosecutor that on this spot your predecessors have resisted the arbitrary power of the Crown, backed by the influence of Crown-serving, time-serving judges!'

There was a grand rustling of judicial ermine at that point, I can tell you! It was my finest moment! I was having the time of my life, believe me, and this was a moment that I was going to seize with all my power, with both hands, and I strained my lungs as I bellowed above the growing pandemonium in the courtroom,

'Tell the prosecutor that though six hundred French bayonets glittered before you, though the roar of French cannon thundered in your ears, you will return a verdict that your own breasts will sanctify, careless whether it pleases a foreign despot or no, or secures or shakes and destroys forever the throne which a tyrant has built upon the ruins of the liberty of a once free and mighty people!'

When I sat down the noise was tremendous and I was bathed in sweat, and shaking. In truth I knew I had staked a man's life upon an enormous gamble: ignore the evidence presented, make no attempt to overturn it, make no plea in mitigation, but merely appeal to the hearts and minds of the jury. A jingoistic gamble with

Bernard's life—and my future career.

But the uproar continued in spite of the overwhelmed ushers; silence fell in the courtroom only when the Clerk of Arraigns called to the jury for their verdict. The foreman stood up. I did not even look at him; I was done.

In a firm tone, the foreman to the jury intoned, 'We find the prisoner not guilty.'

3

There was a moment of stunned silence and then uproar broke loose. The loud shout of exultation began in the gallery where men and women stood up, roaring and fluttering handkerchiefs. Ladies of quality were on their feet hysterically waving their fans—except for two on the bench who had fainted—and Simon Bernard leapt up and shook his fist in triumph to his supporters in the crowd. I was immediately engulfed by a surge of enthusiastic well-wishers scrambling over the benches to embrace me as Lord Chief Justice Campbell rose from his seat, raised his hand, called vainly for silence. But he could not prevent the storm of applause, the hooting, the cheering, the shouting which was soon taken up in the crowded streets outside when news of the verdict reached the assembled throng eager to hear the result.

I was swept out of the courtroom, carried along on a tide of enthusiasm, hats being thrown in the air, street traffic at a standstill and a vast crowd insisted that I be hoisted on a succession of shoulders as I was escorted to Inner Temple Lane. Champagne bottles popped in the street, my name was chanted up and down the alleys and lanes and women threw open casement windows and waved kerchiefs and flags and—in a few cases—petticoats and other items of female apparel. By the time I reached my lodgings I was exhausted.

But next day the storm broke in another direction.

The verdict of *The Times* was that the jury's decision had been a grave mistake. *The Saturday Review* commented gloomily on the effect the decision would have on relations between England and France. Outside England, *L'Univers* snarled that the whole episode was 'disgusting' and *Le Constitutionnel* vilified me personally for my 'calumny and insults against the Emperor'. Nor was the English legal press very happy about the manner in which I had displayed my forensic talents. *The Solicitors' Journal* declared it had formed 'no exalted estimate either of the intelligence of the average English citizen or of the dignity of the English advocate' and other journals such as *The Law Times* and *The Legal Observer* considered my address to the jury as tawdry, inconclusive, offensive in its effrontery, bombastic, blustering and improper! In other words they didn't like it. They claimed I was openly approving assassination as a political solution. They claimed it had been a political speech that swayed the jury, rather than a considered peroration relying on facts in issue and the legal basis of the evidence.

And to some extent I have to admit they were right. On the other hand I had given the jury and the public what they wanted and I had saved Dr Bernard's life. And when an excited, half-inebriated Lord Worsley dragged me out on Friday night to celebrate in Leicester Square we swaggered arm-in-arm to enter the Café Chantant. At that date the café was a popular night house where men and women gathered to smoke cigars, take coffee, eat mutton chops and Welsh rarebits along with pale ale, brandy and gin. We entered the large room, which was furnished in the French style with long mirrors, settees and marble-topped tables and as soon as the French proprietor realized the identity of the hero who had entered he dashed to the piano, mustered the small orchestra and began the singing of *Le Marseillaise*. In a moment all in the room were standing, waving champagne glasses in my direction and singing lustily, roaring out a drunken chorus.

Free champagne was ordered for all—Lord Worsley paid the bill. And the French proprietor knew when he was on to a good thing: next day he issued placards announcing that I would be attending the café again that evening, accompanied by Dr Bernard himself and some of the jurors. In fact none of us actually made an appearance, but the proprietor did a roaring trade nevertheless.

The Bar itself was in turmoil. Some of the young hot-blooded barristers of a radical persuasion held a meeting at St Martin's Hall where one briefless barrister called Slack issued a polemic in favour of rebellion, revolution and regicide. I had sneaked in at the back of the hall but when my presence was noted I was called forward to loud cheering to join the platform party, along with Simon Bernard.

And I fear, a little inebriated, I became somewhat carried away by the occasion. The reporters from *The Daily News* and *The Morning Star* were present, scribbling away industriously, and next day they printed what they claimed I had said,

'It is well known that I rejected the offer of the Crown to prosecute Bernard, a man against whom I believe an unjust and obsolete act of Parliament was put into force! Lord Chief Justice Campbell, as I told him to his face, never dared to tell the jury what an obsolete law it was. . . .'

Next morning, when the effects of the inevitable hangover were still with me I realized I had gone too far by a distance, overstepped the mark, as they say. Spencer Walpole, the Home Secretary, sent me a note, invited me to his chambers and there we had a lively discussion. The Attorney General, pompous Fitzroy Kelly, had a stern word with me. I knew I had to back down and insisted that the newspapers, and particularly *The Morning Star*, had misrepresented what I had said.

I ate the appropriate humble pie in private and consequently when the matter was raised in the House the Home Secretary beat off the charges; Sir James Duke came to my support and

Lord Palmerston spoke valiantly in my defence. I received a stern wigging in private, but they all knew that my speech in the trial had caused a great wash of popular feeling in favour of Bernard, and against any kow-towing to the Emperor of the French. Political advantage could be made of that in due course.

So though the legal press still excoriated me it was another kettle of fish with the public and, equally importantly, with the attorneys. They clamoured to engage me, briefs poured into my chambers, I was called upon to act for aristocrats such as Lady Meux and Lord Dinorban and for less exalted personages such as the moneylender Truelove, an inflammable chemist sued for breach of promise of marriage, and a client who was constantly under the delusion that there was a blue pig under his bed. I gave each my full attention.

I appeared at Carlisle, Liverpool, Chelmsford, York, Guildford and Lancaster and on each occasion the courtroom was crowded with enthusiastic supporters who had come to hear me speak. A horse racing case here, a trespass there—wherever I went it seemed my fame had gone before.

It was a fame the Government could not ignore. They knew they *needed* me.

There was to be a by-election at Reigate and it was intimated to me by Spencer Perceval that I would receive ministerial support if I threw my cap in the ring. I did so.

Unfortunately, it turned out to be a financial fiasco.

After I had once again spent a considerable amount of money in canvassing it emerged that there was some doubt whether the Speaker of the House of Commons had been legally entitled to issue the writ for the by-election and while the wrangling went on I retired in disgust to the summer assizes, then went shooting in Scotland, visited Lord Petre's country seat and then found, late in the day, the Speaker had finally issued the writ.

I dashed back to Reigate at more expense but I faced the

conditions I had seen at Southampton all over again: low class labourers and railway navigators who stormed the doors of the Town Hall, threw fruit and eggs and lighted fireworks and prevented me from speaking. It wasn't political opposition; it was just the effects of drunken mayhem.

I didn't even bother to appear at the hustings.

For I had been warned that Lord Ebrington, MP for Marylebone, might be on the point of relinquishing his seat as a consequence of ill health: in the middle of the Reigate debacle Lord Derby, then Prime Minister, had a conversation with me over cards at Brooks' and I was offered the assistance of others present at the occasion: James Wyld MP, Colonel Dickson and Sir James Duke, all men of influence in the borough.

I realized this was my big chance.

You see, at that time Marylebone was perhaps the most important constituency in England. It was also the most expensive—but I was well known in London, echoes of the Bernard case still resounded in the streets and I had the experience gained at Horsham and Boston behind me. So, encouraged by the Government, I launched myself vigorously into the campaign.

The first thing I did was to get the licensed victuallers on my side by promising to hold my election meetings on their premises. I got the whole of St Pancras up in arms when the Vestry refused me the use of Vestry Hall: I denounced this as an aristocratic plot to keep me—a man of the people—out of Parliament and then I launched into tirades of complaint about political jerrymandering. My opponent was the well-connected Colonel Romilly, who suggested that a straightforward soldier was preferable to a tricky lawyer but that line cut no ice with the electors and I fanned the flames of prejudice and resentment, just as I had in the defence of Simon Bernard. I spoke of secret arrangements in Eaton Square drawing rooms, of aristocrats who wanted to treat Marylebone like a pocket borough, of betrayal of the principles of the Reform Act of 1832. In short, I buried the political promises of Colonel Romilly under a welter of noble aims and principles on my part, I inflamed the minds of my audiences, I persuaded them they were taking part in an event of historic importance.

But I not only brought the electors to a pitch of indignant excitement, I *involved* them, encouraged them, drew them close with my sense of humour. I reminded them that unlike my opponent I actually lived in the borough—albeit as a bachelor. This brought forth ribald comments that on the contrary, I was well known for having at least three 'wives' in Westminster. Of course, this was not far from the truth so I encouraged the laughter, made jokes, brought the wave of feeling to my side.

And at the hustings, on the show of hands I was declared the choice of the voters on the day. A poll was, of course, demanded by Romilly, but as I waited for the result I felt confident: the electoral bruising I had suffered at Horsham, Boston, Hull, Southampton and Reigate could be forgotten.

I had tasted the aperitifs of professional success; now, I knew in my bones that I was about to enjoy the caviar of power.

And so it came about: the most important constituency in England had made up its mind and I was given the majority of the three thousand votes cast.

I remember *The Times* sighing with relief on my behalf. I kept the cutting. Here it is.

'MR EDWIN JAMES QC has been elected for Marylebone by an enormous majority. He has worked long and been rejected often; but his perseverance has received a rich reward at last.'

Rich reward indeed: I saw it as my first step towards a long-anticipated progress to Solicitor General, Attorney General and, eventually, a judge's wig, or the Woolsack itself as Lord Chancellor. Rich reward ... but I have to admit it cost me a great deal to achieve.

How much? Well. . . .

Marylebone was known to be the most expensive borough in England. It was known that the seat had cost Lord Dudley Stuart £7,000 in 1847 while Lord Ebrington had expended £5,000 and Jacob Bell £3,000. *The Times* reckoned it must have cost me at least £5,000. That was, in fact, a considerable underestimate. When all the bills had come in I had to find in excess of £8,000.

How could I afford the enormous expense? I've already intimated, my boy, that I was now among the highest paid advocates of the day. My yearly income was in excess of £7,000 per annum!

You grimace. Well, yes, I agree my earnings, large though they were, could not justify or support such an election expenditure. Also, I was very unlucky. I took my seat in Parliament but only five weeks later, on All Fools Day, a political crisis was reached. Lord Derby, in his minority government, had brought in a Reform Bill. I voted with the majority but in a welter of confusion where no one seemed to know what the result of the vote was, the Bill was regarded as rejected.

Lord Derby immediately resigned. A General Election was called.

So I had to face the electors of Marylebone all over again. And that meant yet another crippling bout of expenditure.

I had good, supportive friends: Sir James Duke, Colonel Dickson, Sir John Shelley, Baron Watson and the other candidate for one of the two seats at Marylebone, Sir Benjamin Hall. They all gathered around to back me but the fight had to begin again. Things were made more difficult by a Tory barrister called Haig who nominated Lord Stanley for the seat, even though it transpired that that gentleman intended standing at King's Lynn. It was nothing more than a scandalous attempt to embarrass the Liberals financially and *The Times* rightly denounced Haig by stating that he was merely out to put the two real candidates—Ben Hall and me—to further expense of canvassing, eating, drinking, agency, carrying and polling.

I was furious, but could do nothing about it—and the expenses mounted again and we dug deeper into our pockets, Ben Hall and I.

I was not really worried about the result. The spectral contender, Lord Stanley, he obtained only 1,083 votes. Sir Benjamin Hall obtained 4,698. As for me, I garnered 5,199 and stood at the head of the poll. I would be a member of the House once more—this time with the possibility of a rather longer tenure.

I was buttonholed later that evening by John Delane, editor of *The Times*, who offered me his hand in congratulation. But looking me in the eye, he remarked, 'You know, James, generally speaking, a man must be either very near a peerage or very near the judicial bench, or very near the Queen's Bench, if he thinks Marylebone a prize worth going for.'

I made no response beyond a knowing smile, but I saw the gleam in his eye and I knew that he was aware soundings had already been made to me by the main men who would take their places in the new government.

'Prince Albert won't like it,' Delane informed me. 'He don't like your style, James.'

Like or not, he wouldn't have been able to stop me, if things had worked out as they were intended to. In the new Government the Lord Chancellor was old; Bethell was Attorney General and Sir Henry Keating was, by all accounts, an incompetent nonentity as Solicitor General. I was assured by those in the know that it would be a matter of months only before I obtained preferment—and the consequent knighthood.

You are still grimacing, young man. You pull a face. Unconvinced, hey? Ah, I understand. It's about the expense. . . .

Yes, I *had* laid out a great deal of money, but I had earned much. I agree, I agree, it could not be enough to bear such expenses, the necessary outgoings for two elections in the space of a few months.

And you're aware I was always somewhat embarrassed financially during the course of my legal career. So you wonder how did I raise the money?

I'm not certain how far I can travel this road, to explain to you. It's a matter of some delicacy and . . . well, although it's all a long time ago now, twenty years and more, and although men have passed on . . . I still feel a little uncertain whether I should tell the story to you.

Ha! I see that now your appetite is really whetted. I'm trapped by my own words. Very well, I suppose after this lapse of time, and in my present circumstances in this near-hovel I inhabit now, it will do no harm to tell you.

It harks back, in a sense, to that meeting in the Abbey Hotel, near Nottingham, on the day my enemy, Lord George Bentinck, died. You will recall that I mentioned to you that among the group called to meet by that rogue, Lewis Goodman, there had been a wealthy banker, a sitting Member of Parliament. His name was John Sadleir. I had not made his acquaintance before that day, but later I came across him from time to time in the Reform Club, for he sat on the Government benches under Lord Aberdeen—Prime Ministers came and went with regularity in those turbulent years. Aberdeen appointed him as a Junior Lord of the Treasury, just a short step from high office.

I knew of him, of course, and of his wealthy reputation: he was said to be fond of drink and ballads, a man occasionally disabled by melancholy like many Irishmen, a one-time notorious faction fighter at the fairs in Kerry and Cork and a sportsman who fancied himself at the sports of football and hurling. But even at the club I met him rarely, and certainly he was not an intimate of mine, so I was surprised when one evening he sent me a note, asked me if I would dine with him. He had hired a private room and the wines served were of excellent quality: as the most successful banker of his day, he was reckoned to be one of the richest, and most personable businessmen in London.

It was only after we had talked politics, eaten a good dinner and were enjoying a brandy and cigar each that I said to him, 'I have the feeling that you have some specific reason for inviting me to dine this evening.'

He smiled. I can see him still, in my mind's eye, a confident, burly, broad-shouldered Irishman, the smoke from his cigar curling softly about his greying, bushy hair, his eyes narrowing slightly as he watched me and I noted the hint of cynicism in his smile.

'I've followed your career with interest, Mr James.'

'Indeed?'

He nodded. 'And I have come to the conclusion that you are an able, courageous man in the courtroom.'

I inclined my head in modest acknowledgment.

'I've also concluded you're a man of few scruples,' he added coolly.

I glared at him, feeling anger rising in my chest at the studied insult. But before I could rise, speak in protest, he leaned forward, holding my glance under a fierce knitting of his brows.

'And you are the man I know I can turn to.'

'Turn to? You are in legal difficulties?' My hackles were up in indignation. 'If you have a legal problem you should talk to your attorneys, discuss it with them, suggest they send instructions to my clerk—'

'No, no!' He waved aside my protest with a dismissive hand. 'This is not something to be discussed with attorneys, or your clerk. It is a private matter. A matter requiring the utmost discretion.'

I waited, not understanding, but vaguely disturbed and, I must admit, strangely on edge.

'So what is it you require of me?' I asked warily.

'In short, James, a certain personal service,' Sadleir said, pausing, and taking a short, suddenly nervous pull at his cigar, 'I want you to assist . . . '

The end of his cigar glowed red.

' . . . I want you to assist me in the matter of my death.'

PART FIVE

1

Chance plays such an important part in men's lives.

Take Carlo Rudio, for instance. You might recall he was one of the bomb-throwers in Paris, the third one to launch his grenade at the Emperor's coach. A great survivor. I first met him, you might be interested to know, in Italy when he was a follower of Garibaldi. And then again, years later in New York when we were together involved in the hunt for President Lincoln's assassin. But I'll tell you about that some other time. Rudio was a remarkable man, a great escapologist. He avoided the death sentence in Paris by blabbing the assassination plot—which resulted in the capture of Orsini and Gomez. He was consequently sent not to the guillotine but to Devil's Island: he was one of the very few who contrived to escape from that hell and he came to live in East London for a while before he emigrated to America. In New York he enlisted in the regular Army, under the name Charles de Rudio and fought in the Civil War. Later, he served as a lieutenant in the Indian wars, with the famous 7th Cavalry under General Custer—and escaped again. He was present at the Little Big Horn, in Benteen's command, and was one of the few to survive the massacre.

Then there's your father. Chance meant that while I knew him in England Rudio knew him in New York, where they were both servicing whores and drilling volunteers in the Civil War.

You know, I saw him recently, your father, that is. It was on the Strand. You don't know a great deal about him, do you? I suppose it's understandable because he was always a committed travelling man—he went to India when he was just nineteen, where he married his first wife, Jane. She's a famous artist now, in Australia, and so is her son, your half-brother. You didn't know that? Jane Stocqueler left your father because she saw little of him after he impregnated her. In the first two years of their marriage he was off for fifteen months travelling in Afghanistan, and she scarcely saw him after that. So she took her son off to Australia. Your own mother, my wife Eliza, she married Stocqueler when she was eighteen—he was forty-seven at the time. He was always partial to young women ... unlike me, for I've always preferred older, more mature ladies: less inane chatter, an understanding of the mechanics of sex and a greater likelihood of gratitude. In fact, I hear your father's just got married again, at the age of sixty-seven. His new wife is thirty, I hear. . . .

But chance meant that your mother Eliza and I would meet; our paths first crossed when she and your father were operating a diorama about the Crimean War in London. A chance meeting ... and then when Eliza and I met again, in New York, chance dictated that she and I were in similar straits: she divorced from your father, who was running around with various ladies and a troop of volunteer horse alongside Rudio; me in the wreckage of my marriage to Marianne Hilliard.

No, no, I'm not prevaricating, don't take me to task with that long face! I'm not really wandering from the point. I *said* I'd tell you about Sadleir, it's just that I'm emphasizing the part chance plays in all our lives.

You see, if Sadleir hadn't glimpsed me at that meeting at the Abbey Inn on the day Lord Bentinck died he wouldn't have formed the swift impression of my character that influenced his decision later. Yes, he might have seen me as a fellow scoundrel from later events but, well, first impressions are important, aren't they?

If only I had ignored Lewis Goodman's summons that day, how different things might have been! It could have been. . . .

What? All right, all right, I'll press on.

That evening in the Reform Club after I'd got over the shock of Sadleir's statement about his desire to die he leaned back comfortably in his chair, watching me with an amused glint in his eyes, and asked, 'What do you know about me, James?'

I took a deep breath, still recovering from the astounding nature of his seemingly casually stated request. 'You're known to be fabulously wealthy.'

He grimaced. 'Go on.'

'You're from Dublin, where you practised as a solicitor—'

'I started in Tipperary, actually, where my father owned a small bank. Moved to Dublin later, before I came to London in 1847. Got elected as member for an Irish seat. What else?'

Carefully, I said, 'You're popular, said to be witty; you're known as a ladies' man and a good dancer.'

'Better than any man of my acquaintance!' he boasted with a laugh. 'Go on! I'm enjoying this!'

'The rest is in the public domain: you're MP for Sligo, Chairman and Director of the London and County Bank—'

'Among others,' he interrupted.

'—and you were a Junior Lord of the Treasury under Lord Aberdeen.' I shrugged. 'You're still an MP. That's about it.'

Sadleir was silent for a little while, contemplating the glowing end of his cigar. At last he looked up at me. 'Since that first brief meeting that time near Welbeck I've watched your career with interest, James. You and I have much in common. You have a similar reputation to mine: you're seen as a witty, popular, successful man. We both enjoy the trappings of success—you live in Berkeley Square now, I believe, while I reside in a mansion in Gloucester Square. We're the darlings of society—we are the recipients of more country house invitations than we can acknowledge. And we have a hunger to rise in life—your father was a humble solicitor, as was mine, but we both are driven by ambition. And there is one other thing we have in common.'

I waited. After a little while, as Sadleir seemed lost in thought, I asked, 'And what other thing do you suggest we have in common?'

He bared his teeth in a mirthless smile. His hand was shaking slightly, and ash fell from the end of his cigar onto the damask cloth on the table. He did not respond to my question immediately. 'We are both *ruthless* in the pursuit of our ambitions.'

I made no demur: it was for him to say what he knew.

'Let me tell you my story,' he said. He stubbed out the cigar and finished the brandy in his glass.

'People are stupid,' he announced. 'They see what they want to see. You know that. I've seen that recognition in your own career. And you've relied upon it—the stupidity of juries, in particular, but also, I hear, of gullible, wealthy ladies and infatuated young men— relied upon it to advance your career. In my case, when I came to London I was armed with the agency of two small banks and was seen at first merely as an Irish adventurer, but as a Member of Parliament—for Carlow in the first instance—I was quickly able to make use of the political and social connections I made and within twelve months, my charm, wit and reputation as a financier gave me entry to a society that included Gladstone, Disraeli, Aberdeen and Sir Robert Peel.' He smiled. 'You knew his brother, I believe.'

I grimaced. 'Colonel Peel? Yes, the *Running Rein* case. People never seem to forget that debacle.'

'The famous Derby fraud. In which our mutual acquaintance, Lewis Goodman, was deeply involved.'

A slow stain of suspicion was beginning to grow in my mind. A suspicion that made me believe that there was indeed much in common between John Sadleir and myself.

He poured himself another brandy, offered me the decanter,

which I accepted.

'As a Parliamentary agent for the Irish banks I made a great deal of tin in those early years,' he explained. 'It enabled me to indulge in speculation, particularly during the railway boom. And believe me, there was a great deal of competition for business in the early days of joint stock banking—all the banks wanted the patronage of the State and there I was, ideally placed, a banker and seated on the Government benches. The financiers, greedy to the very last one of them, sought me out, called for my patronage, and offered me money, money, money. . . .'

Carefully, I murmured, 'You've also built up a reputation as a man of a philanthropic nature.'

'And a good employer. You know, I paid my secretary two thousand a year—mind you, the rogue trebled his income by charging a hundred guineas for each introduction to his master. You can't trust anyone, can you?' He gave a short, barking laugh and sipped at his brandy. 'Yes, I supported many charities, was known to be open-handed for good causes, for was I not reputed to be one of the richest men in London?'

'Rich enough, I heard, to buy thousands of acres in Ireland,' I ventured.

'Indeed.' There was an odd, cynical gleam in his eyes. 'And as a result the Irish farming fraternity clamoured to deposit their money in the Tipperary Bank, once I announced my objective was to buy back large estates for the numerous small tenants. They rushed to invest! Philanthropy, you see! Irresistible! Then there was the publicity, the jostling of journalists seeking an interview: they loved me. As did other writers. Dickens and Thackeray visited the Reform Club once, you know, just to get a glimpse of me, and they sat there smoking and discussing my fabulous wealth. A number of novels—especially Disraeli's—contained thinly veiled portraits of the Honourable Member for Sligo!'

'I've heard you talked about in the Reform Club,' I said quietly, slightly irritated by his boasting.

'As I have you. But it's all smoke and mirrors, ain't it, my learned friend?'

There was a short silence between us as each weighed up the other. At last, in a tight voice, rather strangled voice, I demanded, 'Just what do you mean by that remark?'

He smiled, waved his brandy glass in my general direction.

'Oh, relax, James! You and I both know that wordsmiths like you and me, we can charm birds from trees, money from infatuated women and support from politicians who believe we are men of principle. They don't see what we are in reality. No, before you protest, let me tell you what happened to me. I made use of the contacts I forged in the House and in social circles, everyone believed what they wanted to believe and so much money was pressed upon me that I was able to embark, first of all, on a series of unwise speculations and then, later, a whole range of financial swindles. To the world I was a financial genius; it was thought I was so rich my resources would never be exhausted. But the reality? I never once had the luxury of being really solvent. When I needed money I simply drew it from the Tipperary Bank. From the deposits made by small farmers. Not to invest; just to spend, to maintain the image. And no questions were asked! So by the time I took up the position of Junior Lord of the Treasury I was already deeply in debt. I had issued bogus railway stock; I had mortgaged the Irish landholdings; I had forged land certificates to secure many of my loans, but I was *gambling*, gambling that as a Minister of the Crown I would obtain privileged information that would enable me to recoup my losses by successful Stock Exchange speculation.'

He paused, heaved a theatrical sigh. 'Unfortunately, there were men in the Treasury who were not blinded by my aura of financial invincibility: they began private inquiries and made a report to Lord Aberdeen. He called me in a little while ago. Told me if I did not resign the Treasury, he would publicly remove me.'

This confession had gone far enough to make me nervous. I held up a hand. 'Sadleir, I don't know why you are telling me all this. You must be mad! I could report you to—'

'Not at all, my learned friend. I speak freely because this conversation is subject to legal privilege. You cannot disclose it without my permission.'

'That's nonsense! You're not my client! There's no legal privilege involved!'

Sadleir had the impudence to grin at me. 'Who would believe that, if I claimed that the information I have given you was on a client–legal adviser basis? My dear James, from what I hear you're in enough trouble with the Benchers of the Inner Temple as it is! A dispute about whether you're my counsel or not? I'm sure your enemies would be delighted to have another stick to beat you with.'

I stood up, pushing back my chair. 'That's enough! I'll listen to no more of this. I give you my assurance that I won't repeat the conversation but—'

'Please sit down, my friend. Hear me out.' There was a sudden, steely edge to his voice.

'To what purpose?' I spat at him. 'This conversation is dangerous—it's already gone further than it should.'

'To what purpose, you ask?' He took out another cigar, lit it, puffed contentedly and sent out a spiral of smoke into the air. 'Purpose? Why, the furtherance of your ambition.'

I stood rooted to the spot, staring down at him. He leaned forward, refilled my glass from the decanter and gestured towards the seat I had just vacated. 'Sit down, James. Be sensible. Accept that I've recognized in you some of the desires that have burned in me.'

'I don't know what you're talking about. You've admitted to me you're a fraud and a thief! To compare us—'

'*Sit down,*' he insisted coldly. 'Don't ride the high horse so indignantly! It doesn't become you. My life has been one of pursuit of money, women—and high office. How are you so different? I *know* you, James. While I once hoped to become Chancellor of the Exchequer—imagine what that would have meant for me—I've no doubt you look forward and dream of the day you'll become Lord Chancellor. For me, the Exchequer is lost. For you . . . all is still possible. Except—and it's a big exception—*you can't afford to pay the price.'* His glowing eyes were fixed on mine. 'But perhaps we can do something about that.'

My heart was thudding in my chest. I knew it was foolish of me to remain there, but in spite of logic, I resumed my seat, reached for the brandy glass, downed the burning liquid, searing the back of my throat.

'To reach the heights of your ambition, my learned friend, you need to obtain a seat in Parliament. You have friends and supporters, and the Liberal Party to back you but . . . you lack the cash that would put you in the House. Don't talk to me of your earnings! I know of the liabilities under which you labour! I know of your indebtedness to Lewis Goodman and the way in which your paper floats about among half the moneylenders in London! I know of your extravagance, your social climbing. I tell you, man, I *know* you, I *recognize* you, and I appreciate your problems! Because we are brothers under the skin!' He paused, almost glaring at me. 'But even though my own cause is lost, I can help *you* make the final push. I can finance you. I can help you attain your greatest ambitions!'

Contemptuously, and yet a little breathlessly, I snarled, 'Money? Help me? You've already confessed to me that you're insolvent.'

'That doesn't mean I can't lay my hand on a considerable amount of money.'

I was breathing hard. The devil of temptation burned in my chest. I could hardly believe what I was hearing, that the confessions of this financial giant were so heinous, that his attitude was so nonchalant but I was hooked by the bait he seemed to be dangling. In the silence that followed, John Sadleir watched me with care as the blue cigar smoke curled about his head.

'In just one week's time,' he murmured at last, 'the Tipperary Bank will fail. That failure will be rapidly followed by the collapse of a small bank at Newcastle-on-Tyne, and then, most likely, the banking giant London and Capital will go to the wall. There will be much wailing in the City. Collapse of large companies. And no doubt a number of suicides.'

'How can you be certain?' I demanded.

'I have drawn a cheque on the last named bank. This morning they have refused to pay: they will soon announce the reason: in the City everyone will then be made aware of the fact that there are no funds available in my account. The news will spread. There will be a rush upon the banks. It will be disclosed that my debts amount to almost three hundred thousand pounds. I will be ruined; thousands of shareholders in the banks will be ruined.' He paused, watching me with a cynical gleam in his eyes. 'On the other hand you, of course, *you* may well profit.'

'What do you mean?'

'Think of the deluge of cases that will be brought in the courts! There's enough work there to last for a decade at least. And aren't you one of the leading members of the Bar as far as bankruptcy cases are concerned?'

He was right, of course.

'Not that the vast income you'll receive from such briefs will help you much in your ambitions. The money will come in slowly. What you need is an immediate injection of cash. Money that can be used to buy yourself a seat in Parliament.'

I could not resist the obvious question. 'So what do you—facing ruin—intend to do?'

He was silent. His face had paled somewhat but his voice was strong and controlled. 'Intend to do? I've already told you. I need to die, after writing the appropriate letter, of course. Die, by my own hand. I have it all planned. Or most of it. The means, the location .... There is just one more piece to put in place.'

'Me?' I guessed. 'But how can I . . . assist in your death?'

'I need you to identify the corpse that will be found on Hampstead Heath next Saturday morning.'

My hand was shaking when I reached again for the brandy decanter. We had dined well, the wines had been of good vintage and I had now taken several measures of brandy but I did not feel inebriated. My mind was whirling, questions turned and clashed in my mind and I still could not quite understand what Sadleir expected of me. But the glimmerings were there, the chinks of light in the darkness.

'Today,' he said quietly, 'I drew £14,000 from my account in the Tipperary Bank. If you agree to identify my corpse next Saturday, I will pay you £8,000. Cash. Immediately. I know I can trust your word as a gentleman to keep to your side of the bargain if I pay you the money in advance.'

I was aware of the irony in his words. But suspicion was hardening in my chest. 'The corpse I identify—'

'Will not be mine, naturally.'

The silence grew around us, extended. Faintly I heard the chimes of a distant clock on the night air. I shivered. 'But how can you possibly arrange that?' I protested weakly.

'There is a surgeon at Guy's Hospital who will be ... accommodating. We have an understanding. Of a financial nature, of course. He has already identified a likely candidate who resembles me in height, weight. These things are easily arranged, you may be surprised to hear. Or perhaps not. Surgeons have long dealt in a morbid traffic in the dead, haven't they, ever since the days of Burke and Hare?'

I took a deep breath. 'Why do you wish to involve me?'

'Respectability.' He almost sneered the word. 'A fellow lawyer.

A fellow Liberal. A fellow member of the Reform Club. Your word, as a popular Queen's Counsel, a man of note, will be accepted. Of course, you will not be alone. I have already arranged for another person of *reputation* to stand beside you in the identification.'

'But won't there be an attempt to call members of your family to make an identification?' I argued feebly.

'My brother has gone to Ireland. There are no other relatives. No, I have arranged that the authorities will seek no persons to view the corpse, other than two respectable members of the Reform Club. That will suffice.'

I sat for several minutes in silence. Sadleir made no further attempt to persuade me. He merely waited. And it is true: he *did* know me. He knew of my financial state; he knew of my desires; and perhaps he was right in his estimation of my character, my burning ambitions, my lack of scruples.

My mouth was dry. 'When did you first decide to contact me for this . . . purpose?'

He shrugged. 'I told you. The first time we met at the Abbey Inn that day, it laid a foundation. You were involved with Goodman: he thought you might be interested in his proposition that day. The simple fact that he thought you might join in with the proposal he was about to make gave me a perspective regarding your character. I duly noted that fact—even if the proposition he made that day did not come to fruition. Now, some years later, and having followed your career, realized the extent of your ambition, I knew that you'd be the right man to approach.'

And he was right. In a flare of decision I sat up, held his glance firmly. I took a deep breath. 'To do what you ask . . . I'd want the whole fourteen thousand.'

He shook his head. 'Impossible. I will shortly be on a boat bound for Valparaiso and I need something to pay for my immediate passage. The most I can offer is ten thousand.'

We finally settled on an immediate payment of £12,000.

2

I was in a highly nervous state as I waited in the Reform Club the following Sunday morning. It was a bitterly cold day. The Serpentine had frozen over again—it had already happened the previous November—and there were more than two inches of ice on the Long Waters at Kensington Gardens. I heard someone say in the club that there were upwards of three hundred skaters on the Lower Pond that morning. And other stories had already begun to circulate: there was a rumour that the body of a gentleman had been discovered by a passing labourer, near Jack Straw's Tavern on Hampstead Heath. The body had been convulsed, the face contorted into a mask of pain. Nearby lay a discarded silver mug, probably flung away in death agonies. In the pocket of the corpse had been found an empty bottle that had contained prussic acid. There was also a letter. The whispers were circulating that the corpse was that of a man of public reputation, and the lifeless body was being held by the police in the dead house, for positive identification before further information was released.

The police constable arrived at the Reform Club late that morning.

I was alone in the library, an unread newspaper in my shaking hand when he was shown in by the porter; he entered, varnished hat in hand, respectful in demeanour. 'Mr James? There has been a discovery of a body on Hampstead Heath. Identification is required. The Commissioner has requested that I ask for your assistance in the matter. Would you be able to accompany me to the dead house, sir?'

A surgeon at Guy's Hospital, I thought, now the Commissioner himself. I wondered at what level their remuneration had been settled. Sadleir had certainly prepared the ground well. But just how well was yet to be revealed to me: when I arrived at the dead house—there was only one mortuary in London at that time—I was shown to a small waiting room in the dreary low-roofed building next to the hospital. There was another person already seated there. He did not rise, or attempt to speak to me, though when he glanced up, coughing into a kerchief, he favoured me with a brief nod.

With a feeling of shock, I recognized him at once. The eminent Dr Thomas Wakley.

Wakley had been known as a bare-fist fighter in his youth and throughout his career had been noted for his aggressive, bustling personality, but he was now a pale shadow of the man he had been. He was famous, of course, for being the surgeon who had founded the medical journal *The Lancet*, he had served as a Radical MP for a period and had conducted some notable campaigns on medical and political matters over the years. He had long argued for the establishment of a system of coroners and when that battle had been won he himself had been the first to be appointed coroner, at Finsbury. But when I stared at him that morning I saw an elderly, lank-haired, grey-bearded individual racked with consumption, crouched over his sputum-stained handkerchief, his skin pale, almost transparent and his eyes milky with pain.

But his name—in view of his reputation—would be of significant importance when added to mine as an identifier of the corpse of John Sadleir, the banker MP.

Someone else entered the room behind me. I turned, and to

my surprise recognized the police inspector well acquainted with me and my history: Inspector Redwood had seemed to dog my footsteps over the years. Now, he seemed as surprised as I to meet. He glanced past me towards Wakley, frowned, then after a moment's hesitation he handed me a piece of paper. I recall the manner in which he studied me with some curiosity as I read the handwritten suicide note.

'I cannot live. I have ruined too many. I could not live and see their agony. I have committed diabolical crimes unknown to any human being. They will now appear, bringing my family and others to distress, causing to all shame and grief that they should never have known. I blame no one but attribute all to my own infamous villainy. . . .'

I did not need to read more: after all, I had helped Sadleir compose the missive which was to be found on the corpse on Hampstead Heath. I looked up: Redwood was still staring at me, a strange, uncertain light in his eyes.

The police constable who had summoned me from the Reform Club spoke to Wakley in a subdued tone. The frail old man nodded, rose to his feet and then shuffled away with the officer into the adjoining room in the dead house. I waited, holding Redwood's glance with all the coolness I could summon in spite of the thudding of my heart.

'Mr James,' Redwood murmured at last, almost to himself. 'Death seems to ride upon your shoulder.'

I frowned. 'What's that supposed to mean?'

His features were impassive. 'As I recall, we first met when that unfortunate girl was pulled from the Thames some years ago. The suicide, we assumed. A girl known to you. Then it was you who later reported the discovery of that body in the sewers—the body the Commissioner ordered us to make no further inquiries about. And then, well, I'm still wondering about the events surrounding the death of Lord George Bentinck, and whatever part you might have played in it—'

'He died of natural causes,' I snapped angrily, 'and it was nothing to do with me!'

'So you've said before now. And here you are today, turning up to identify the body of a dead man, a suicide on Hampstead Heath.'

I still held his glance firmly. I handed the suicide letter back to him. 'This communication seems to explain everything. Clearly *felo de se*. I am merely here, summoned to help identify the corpse for formal purposes.'

The door to the other room opened and Wakley and the police constable returned. The constable glanced apologetically at Inspector Redwood and then looked at me. 'Mr James?'

I turned away from Redwood and followed the other officer into the cold room where the corpse was lying. It was a long whitewashed place with a stone-flagged floor, dimly lit with a pale wintry light filtering through high windows. A series of tables extended the length of the room, on which had been placed corpses, covered with sheets. One only was exposed and the constable led me towards that particular table.

'Dr Wakley has already given his statement. Are you also able to make an identification, sir?' he asked in a low, respectful tone.

I still recall the sweet, disgusting odour of advancing putrefaction in that room, the coldness of the atmosphere, and the sight of the twisted body lying on the table. The spine was bent, the body curled in foetal agony, and the features were scarred with a fearful pain, the mouth tortured, the eyes rolled up, one hand seeming still to claw at the cheeks as the infernal pain had torn the life from his body. The dying man had suffered. The prussic acid had done its job well. I nodded.

'That is John Sadleir,' I said, hesitating momentarily, still staring at the corpse. The mysterious surgeon at Guy's Hospital had chosen the victim well: the body was of the height of Sadleir, the hair of a similar colour. For the rest, the face was so frozen and twisted as to be almost unrecognizable.

I returned to the other room. Thomas Wakley was seated at a small desk, signing some formal papers presented to him by Redwood. As I waited my turn I wondered about the old man coughing there over the documents. Many times since that day I have considered what part Wakley must have played in that charade, and why. He was a man of great reputation. I knew why I was there, but Thomas Wakley? Perhaps it was the debts he had accumulated—for during his career he had been a most litigious man, being involved in numerous libel suits. And years ago there had been that business of an insurance claim that the company had failed to pay out after the fire at his premises, started, he claimed by the Thistlewood gang. Maybe he really *did* believe that the corpse on the table that February morning was that of his fellow member of the Reform Club; maybe it was just that he was swayed by the fact of the letter that had been found on the body.

Or maybe this former coroner had been chosen because he was old, frail, consumptive with fading eyesight and intellect. Indeed, he was to die not long after this identification. I never did reach any conclusion in my own mind as to why he had been there at my side that day in the dead house, what invitation he had been responding to. . . .

The story of John Sadleir's last hours appeared in the newspapers over the next few days as the details slowly emerged. It was reported that he had eaten dinner on Saturday night at his home in Gloucester Square, attended by his butler. He had earlier despatched a servant to a local chemist for a bottle of prussic acid, ostensibly for the use of the stud groom at Sadleir's other house at Leighton Buzzard. Between dinner and midnight Sadleir had sat alone in his drawing room, writing two letters. And when the servants had retired for the night he had stolen from the house, taking the bottle of poison and a silver mug and walked to Jack Straw's Tavern. There under a clear sky on the frosty Heath he had filled the mug with the prussic acid and drained it, ending his life.

And now, he was officially dead.

But I knew he was on a boat, bound for Valparaiso.

His prediction about the legal storm that would be unleashed after his 'suicide' was correct. Over the next year a rash of cases was brought in the courts consequent upon the failure of the Tipperary Bank, in which thousands of Irish farmers were ruined. I received instructions in a considerable number of the actions and my income soared enormously that year. As for the twelve thousand he had given me, that I secreted away, squirreled in an oak chest, my war chest, ready for the day when a seat became available to me. I still borrowed money to pay off my earlier, regularly mounting debts but I knew I would need cash and a significant amount if I were successfully to contest a seat in Parliament. The oak treasure chest remained locked in my chambers, it was my secret hoard.

In the event it was not nearly enough, as I've already intimated to you, but early availability of such an amount of cash enabled me to confidently borrow further in the market as the election expenses mounted. I could not possibly have managed otherwise. So it was really John Sadleir's cash, the result of his fraudulent behaviour that funded my success, in my scramble for a seat the House of Commons.

And I *was* a success, even though there will be many now who would claim I had failed as a Parliamentarian. I still have enemies!

I took my seat proudly as representative of the great Borough of Marylebone, all upright respectability in my dark suit, stiff black satin tie with a rigorously decorous demeanour to match. The Duke of Cambridge himself sat under the clock that evening; Earl Grey, Earl Granville, the Bishop of Oxford, the Earl of Hardwicke were there, as were Prussian and Sardinian ministers along with other members of foreign powers. For the occasion of my swearing-in coincided with a debate on a new Reform Bill.

I made my maiden speech that very night and it caused a considerable sensation not least because I called the Bill a sham and a delusion but I announced I meant to speak what I believed to be the truth. And I voted with the majority to defeat the Bill. So, when Lord Derby's government then fell, within five weeks of my election, I was able to claim to the electorate when I stood again that I had voted with my conscience.

At the second election my supporters made much of my experiences in the courts: I was the eloquent exposer of Army maladministration—in reference to my withering cross-examination of Lord Lucan—and the glorious defender of Dr Simon Bernard. And as I've told you I was re-elected, top of the poll, with Sir Benjamin Hall as my stable-mate. Sadleir's war chest had all but gone by that point. Nevertheless, my prospects were glittering.

Socially, I was even more sought after: there were private dinner parties in Berkeley Square, invitations to shooting parties in Norfolk and Scotland, and the State Dinner at the Albion in Aldersgate Street. Eulogies appeared in *The Illustrated London News* and the *Monmouthshire Merlin*. Briefs cascaded into my chambers: I acted in cases involving cock-fighting contests, reputations of actresses, the sale of Army commissions, trespass and breach of promise. And I forced myself upon the attention of the Government: one month I spoke fifteen times, the next month eight. I did not confine myself to legal topics but spoke on public health, weights and measures, the Royal Parks, the cleaning of the Serpentine and Crinan Canals. On Derby Day I rose to propose the House adjourn to enable members to attend at Epsom. And I even spoke on bribery and corruption.

The House enjoyed my jokes. When I fought passionately for the Licensed Victuallers against the import of cheap, adulterated continental wines I was able to announce that 'I hope the Government will at least stand by the British quart—if not, I shall certainly make a *pint* of doing so!' I drew admiration from the press and backslapping tributes from the publicans. I took up the rights of workers in the building industry—there were some five thousand men out of work in St Pancras alone—and I was regarded as the architect of the establishment of the London Trades Council. And I took up the cause of Garibaldi, seeking to unify Italy and bring down the Bourbons in Naples. So the Government was well aware of my presence and my energy, my wit and passion, my commitment and burning oratory and I was quietly informed that my name was to go forward to become the next Solicitor General, with a consequent knighthood.

Punch crowed, and predicted I would eventually become '*LORD FITZEDWIN, the new Lord Chancellor.*'

But . . . it never happened. I was struck down by my enemies. The mere thought now still embitters me, even after all these years. The glittering prizes lay tantalizingly within my grasp and all would have been well until . . . well, until that damnable accident in Canada, when the steamer *Lady Elgin* collided with a schooner, the *Milwaukee*, on Lake Superior. Both ships foundered.

I was in Naples with Garibaldi when the news came through. I did not know of it at the time but one of the men who drowned that fateful day was Herbert Ingram, the proprietor of *The Illustrated London News*, who over the years had supported me in more ways than one. And when I returned to England, to continue my duties as Recorder of Brighton and Member for Marylebone I was not aware that Ingram's executor was going through the dead man's private papers . . . and discovering information to my discredit.

But the memories are too painful, and I am tired. I'm not a young man any more, you know; I'm approaching seventy and a long discourse like this, even recounting my glory days, it exhausts me.

You look out of sorts. You're pulling a face.

No, I'm not being evasive. I *will* talk of my fall, but another time, perhaps tomorrow, but for the moment—

You are still not satisfied! Ah, you feel I have been avoiding an issue I have mentioned several times. It has not been deliberate, I assure you. Have I not told you the truth about John Sadleir's death? After all this time? But it's *Bentinck* you want to hear about. My enemy, Lord George Bentinck and his demise on that fateful day when I first met Sadleir, at Lewis Goodman's meeting at the Abbey Inn, near Welbeck.

All right, before I retire for the night I'll tell you.

3

When a prisoner is found guilty of a serious offence such as forgery he is likely at some stage to find himself in Pentonville, almost certainly Newgate, until finally he's moved along to be incarcerated in one of the prison hulks on the Thames. Edward Agar had been held in both Pentonville and Newgate, prior to his transportation to Australia—awaiting suitable transport, it seems.

You'll recall Edward Agar. I had acted for him, at Lewis Goodman's request, years earlier. And he had been present that day at the Welbeck Inn.

I naturally had occasion from time to time to visit the prisons, usually to interview prisoners like Dr Simon Bernard who would be committed to Newgate or some other place of incarceration while awaiting trial on the Queen's Bench, or the Court of Sessions, or the Central Criminal Court—the Old Bailey.

Some time before I took my seat in Parliament, I was paying such a professional visit to Newgate to interview a client whose instructions I had received through Mr Fryer, the rascally attorney who had taken a lease for me at 27, Berkeley Square—and had, incidentally, lent me over £20,000, in the cheerful belief that he might thus have a future Lord Chancellor in his clutches with a likely huge future financial return. But that's another matter.

I had concluded my business with my client—at this distance

of time I've no recollection who he was—and was making my way back towards the main gates when one of the warders stopped me in the inner courtyard, laying a hand on my arm. I glared at him and he quickly removed his impertinent fingers. He grimaced.

'Mr James? A word, if you please, sir.'

His tone was respectful enough.

'What is it?'

'There's a prisoner, sir. He's heard that you're visiting one of the cells. He's asked me to request that you spare him a few minutes. He wishes to discuss something with you.'

Somewhat irritated at the presumption, I said, 'If he wants to talk with me he should make an approach through his attorney. I don't have time—'

'He's most insistent, Mr James. He says it's a matter of urgency. He says you know him . . . and some of his *friends*.'

The turnkey eyed me boldly. Men like this warder, they could make an additional living from the favours they bestowed on prisoners in their care: it always surprised me how money could so freely flow in and out of prison, along with pornography, food, drink, opium and a battalion of low-class whores. But it was the unsubtle reference to *friends* that held my attention. I had spent enough time with denizens of the underworld, in a professional capacity as well as rubbing shoulders with them in gambling houses, pugilistic encounters and race meetings, to be aware that it could be dangerous to ignore the wishes of some of those men who were sometimes designated as members of the 'flash mob'.

'Who is this man who wishes to talk with me?' I demanded irritably.

'Edward Agar. He was convicted of forgery and passing false cheques. He's awaiting transportation. Due for the hulks at Portland any day now.'

I hesitated. I was reluctant to go back down to the cells, but on the other hand I was a little intrigued. Agar must know I would be able to do nothing for him, a convicted criminal; there was no appeal system under which I could assist him. But the turnkey had suggested the man had an urgent matter to discuss.

Curiosity got the better of me. I nodded. 'All right. I'll give him a few minutes of my time.'

The warder led me back into the forbidding building. A few moments later, after traversing the echoing corridor the cell door was thrown open and I entered. The iron door clanged shut behind me. I found myself in a narrow, damp-smelling room separated from Newgate Street by a thick stone wall. Dim light filtered through a high window overlooking the inner courtyard that housed the gallows on which many notorious criminals had met their end.

The man who faced me scarcely resembled the individual I had known. Imprisonment had diminished him. He no longer wore the trappings of his trade, elegant clothing, well-groomed whiskers, smart appearance: the coarse clothing of the prisoner's garb made him seem smaller and less imposing. But it was not just his general appearance: his hair was greying, his lined features were considerably leaner, cheeks fallen in, his despairing shoulders were hunched and there was a haunted look about his deep-set eyes.

'So, Agar,' I said coldly enough, 'they've done for you at last.'

His narrow head came up, and for a moment a flash of his old confident arrogance came back. 'Oh, they caught me to rights, Mr James. So I've no regrets. I been at the trade for years. My only regret is there were a few years when I went straight. Waste of time, that was.'

'And now your time is destined to be spent in Australia.'

'That's what I wanted to see you about, Mr James.'

'It's too late to ask for my help. I assisted you once before, at Lewis Goodman's request. But he's left the scene for France. I wasn't involved at your trial, and I can't do anything for you now. This meeting indeed, it's quite irregular—'

'It's not me I want to talk about, sir. It's Fanny.'

'Who?'

'Fanny Kay. My woman. They're not treating her right. Not like they promised. And the child has died. She's desperate. Living in poverty. And in a few days I'll be in the hulks, then Australia!'

I was silent for a few moments, staring at him. If he thought that in my capacity as a lawyer I could help him, or his woman, he was mistaken. She would be a matter for the Parish, the Poor Law.

'I don't see how I can be of assistance,' I said brusquely and turned to leave. His next words riveted me to the spot.

'I'll talk about the gold bullion robbery, Mr James. I'll tell how it was done. And I'll tell who did it. I'll tell *everything*.'

The words hit me like a blow between the shoulder blades. I turned slowly to face Agar.

'The gold bullion robbery?'

You surely must have heard about that event, my boy! It was the sensation of Europe! But . . . ah, I see, you were on the high seas, the *Bella*, on the Australian run. So the details never reached you at the time.

It was gold bullion, destined for the Crimea, for the pay of the troops. There were regular payments sent out, via Paris. This particular consignment was due for transfer in May 1855. As I recall from the newspapers at the time the gold was packed into three boxes by the firm of Abell, Spielman and Bell. The boxes, which were bound with hoops of iron, locked with Chubb locks and sealed, were transferred to the South Eastern Railway Company. Keys to the boxes were held only by senior railway officials, and by the captain of the Channel steamer, the *Lord Warden*.

It seems the sealed, iron-bound boxes were placed in the guard's van and taken by rail to Folkestone. From there they were shipped to Boulogne, where the boxes were weighed. It was noted there was some slight discrepancy in weight from the original manifesto but nevertheless the boxes, still sealed, were transferred by rail to

Paris. It was there that the boxes were opened. They were found to contain not gold bullion, but lead shot! You can imagine the outcry, and the manhunt that was then launched. The British government claimed the gold must have been abstracted in France; the French government howled it must have been stolen in England. No one wanted to accept responsibility. Intensive investigations were undertaken, private detectives employed, railway workers and company employees questioned but all to no avail. It was as though the bullion had vanished into thin air—and there were no suspects identified, no theories as to how the gold could have been taken from iron-bound, sealed boxes—not even where the theft might have taken place.

Hundreds of people were interviewed, the months dragged by and the whole event remained a mystery. The police were helpless; the railway company was overwhelmed with anxiety; questions were asked about the Chubb locks, the security system—the honesty of railway employees. But no one could discover who had committed the crime, not even suggest *how* the job had been done.

And now here I found myself in a Newgate cell with a self-confessed and notorious forger due to be transported to Australia telling me he could hand me the key that would unlock the mystery of the missing Crimean gold bullion!

'*You* were involved in the robbery?' I demanded incredulously.

Edward Agar's lean features were hollowed with anxiety as he stared at me, almost pleading. 'He promised me he would give my share to Fanny. He said he would look after her, after my arrest. He *promised* me!'

'Who are you talking about?'

'That damned rogue Pierce!'

I took a deep breath. 'You'd better tell me the whole story. From the beginning.'

'You'll make sure Fanny will be looked after? You promise me you'll do what you can; promise me on the word of a gentleman?'

'Tell me what you know,' I replied grimly, still only half believing he had anything of worth to disclose.

Agar was silent for a while, almost gulping for breath as though overcome with panic, or disappointment, or fury at the manner in which he felt he had been betrayed. And then he told me.

'It was my idea from the start—it was after I came back from America and business in Australia that I conceived the plan. The regular transport of the bullion to the Crimea: it was well known. So I planned, first, by recruiting a man called Pierce, who worked as a printer for the railway company. He introduced me to a railway guard called Burgess, who he claimed would be able to obtain impressions of the keys to the bullion boxes. Pierce and I, we personally checked the systems used, followed several consignments to Folkestone, even raised suspicions among watching police—who thought we might be pickpockets! So Pierce and I we split up after that. And Burgess recruited a third member of the group: George Tester, a clerk in the railway superintendent's office.' An element of faded pride entered his tone. 'It was Tester who allowed me entry to the office where the bullion safe keys were held: I took wax impressions. Also I did a calculation, worked out the comparative weight of the bullion—to have ready its equivalent in lead shot.'

Impatiently, I said, 'So that was how you planned it. But how did you *effect* the robbery without disclosure?'

Agar leaned his head back against the damp wall of his cell. He sounded weary suddenly. 'We bought the lead shot to the estimated required weight. We packed carpet bags with the shot, concealed them under our cloaks as we took first class tickets to Folkestone. Dressed like gentlemen, we were. We boarded the train carrying the bullion in the guard's van. The guard was Burgess.'

His voice trembled but he rallied and a hint of pride came into his tone. 'In the confusion at the London Bridge stop I left Pierce in first class and entered the guard's van. When we moved off,

Burgess assisted me as I broke into the first bullion box with a mallet and chisel, to remove the iron hoops. Then I used the copied keys. We removed the bullion, replaced it with lead shot and when we arrived at the Redhill stop Pierce joined us in the van. We then attacked the second and third boxes—the third held smaller bars, of Californian gold. We replaced the iron binding, relocked the boxes, now filled with lead shot, and used a wax taper to reseal the locks.'

I was still sceptical. 'But how did you remove the gold from the train?' I asked.

'Confusion again at Folkestone. Pierce and I left the van before the boxes were unloaded. We rejoined the first class carriages, took tickets onwards to Dover, carrying the carpet bags with us while the bullion boxes were taken aboard the steamer. We celebrated that afternoon with champagne, in the Dover Castle Hotel before taking the train back to London the same day. By the time they weighed the boxes in Boulogne, and opened them in Paris, we had long since dispersed. To all extents and purposes, the gold had vanished into thin air. And so had we.'

I was silent for a little while, staring fixedly at Agar, wondering whether I was hearing the truth. But his tone rang with a wearied sincerity.

'And afterwards?' I inquired.

'We shared out the gold—more or less equally, between me, Burgess and Pierce. Tester got paid off. I started the process of melting it down. Saward—Jem the Penman—he helped at the beginning in selling some of the gold. That was before he was taken up, with me, for passing forged cheques. He's already been transported; I'll be next. That's why I need your help now, Mr James! Once I'm in the hulks, or on the high seas to the Australia penal colony, what chance will I have to get back at Pierce? What chance will Fanny Kay have? Pierce should have kept his promise: if he'd done right by Fanny I'd have taken my medicine and kept mum. But he broke his promise—he left the child to die, and Fanny to starve! He's given her nothing—*nothing*! But he promised!'

And I gave my promise.

I kept out of the business, of course: I could not afford to have my name linked in any way to this affair. So the following day I contacted Ben Gully. He went to see Fanny Kay, and then arranged for her to meet Mr Rees, the solicitor to the South Eastern Railway who had taken a personal interest in the matter and publically vowed to pursue the miscreants who had robbed the Folkestone train.

A year later it was all over. The jury took only ten minutes in the Old Bailey to convict the robbers: after testimony from the embittered Agar and Fanny Kay, Burgess was sentenced to transportation for fourteen years; Tester received a similar sentence and Pierce was jailed for larceny. Agar, of course, gained no mercy or credit for his testimony: he was still transported to Australia, where Saward, his co-conspirator and old criminal acquaintance was already serving his sentence. But only part of the proceeds of the robbery were ever recovered.

I know, I know, I've told you this story as it happened, but of course what you want to know is about the mysterious death of Lord George Bentinck. But you see, it's all part of the same history. Before I left the Newgate cell that day I pressed Edward Agar for the full story.

'Did the bullion robbery have anything to do with that meeting Lewis Goodman held at the Abbey Inn near Welbeck, those years ago? Goodman spoke of an *investment*. Saward was there, wasn't he, and you—'

'And a banker called Sadleir,' Agar affirmed. 'The man who topped himself recently. Yes, Mr James, the meeting was about what I just told you—Saward and Goodman were involved, raising some cash for the putting up of the plot—we needed money, naturally, to set up the whole scheme. Burgess, Tester, Pierce, they all needed tin in advance to do the planning, pay some bribes.'

'But why was I invited that day?' I queried.

Agar shrugged. 'Goodman's idea. He teased you, asking for money for an investment—the robbery—but really he wanted you there as a reliable adviser, a legal contact, a backup in case of trouble. Someone he could put pressure on later in court, if things started to go awry. But then it all went wrong right away, when his lordship walked in. He saw us all together. Me, Sadleir, Goodman, Saward—and you! It meant Goodman pulled out, Sadleir pulled out—and you, Mr James, well, you really were never in it at all, were you?'

I took a deep, quivering breath. I remembered the sudden panic in that taproom, when Bentinck made his remark and turned on his heel.

'That leaves me with one question. What actually happened to Lord George Bentinck that day?'

Edward Agar's features were in shadow, and his tone was low, his voice so quiet that I had to strain to hear him distinctly. 'When he caught us there, recognized some of us, made that remark about rogues, he caused consternation. You, I recall, you were for chasing after him to remonstrate but Goodman held you back. And Sadleir, he was really panicked. From what I hear now he had good reason: he must already have been stealing money from his banks, and if Bentinck started talking about him and the company he was keeping his reputation might have suffered, his stock might have gone down, questions might have been asked about his activities, and expenditures.'

'I wanted to follow Bentinck. Goodman held me back,' I said woodenly.

'But Sadleir plunged out into the wood, after Bentinck. Goodman gave me the nod and I followed them. I stayed at the edge of the woods and I saw Sadleir catch up with his lordship, saw their argument on the path. I couldn't hear what was being said, but Sadleir grabbed at Bentinck's arm. His lordship turned on him angrily and they exchanged high words. I don't know what was said, and I kept myself half-hidden among the trees but I saw his lordship, enraged, face suffused with blood—he was always a quick-tempered man, I heard. He raised his stick, swung it at Sadleir's head. Sadleir ducked, the blow missed, and then Sadleir let him have it with a straight left. He'd been a fair pugilist, I hear, back in Ireland as a young man. Fought at the county fairs. Certainly, it was a well-struck blow. It took Lord George high on the chest, and he went down like a stone.'

Agar sighed, and shook his head.

'Just the one blow, it was. Sadleir stood there for a little while, staring down at his lordship, who hadn't moved. Then he sort of stiffened, looked about him—he didn't see me skulking among the trees—and he set off briskly, back down the track in the direction of Thoresby. He didn't return to the Abbey Inn. I never actually saw him again. He took no part in the robbery planning thereafter. Nor did Goodman—he chased off to France, after his daughter, seduced she was by some French count.'

So there you have it, Joe my boy.

One blow—the coroner found an unexplained bruise on Lord George's chest, but there was no explanation for it and so he concluded Bentinck had died of a heart attack. There was no reason for Sadleir to come forward—and every reason not to. Some suspicion lurked in the mind of the police, especially Inspector Redwood, but he never found any evidence to connect me with the incident—it's been suspicion only. Breaths of suspicion. . . .

And after hearing the truth from Agar, I had no reason ever to talk about it. Until today: and this is a private family conversation, ain't it? Sadleir ended an alleged suicide, there was no one who would want to talk about the meeting at the Abbey Inn and all Redwood's suspicions would come to naught.

So . . . my worst enemy had passed on . . . not that it made much difference to me in the long run. I was soon making enemies enough, if only through envy of my professional success, my rise to become a Recorder, a QC, an MP, and, well, my financial indebtedness, which continued to rise and rise and rise.

But it was a dead man who enabled me to obtain my goal: a seat in Parliament. There were occasional rumours, of course—it was said from time to time that someone resembling John Sadleir had been seen in Quito, or Valparaiso, or in some remote town in the Andes. But nothing was proved. And as we learned recently in the Tichborne Claimant trial, a man can vanish among those southern hills. Oddly enough, Sadleir's brother, who had been involved in his crimes, had fled to Switzerland where he was murdered some years later. A botched attempt at robbery, it seems: he died for a fob watch. Chance again, hey?

But now, I must insist, I'm an old man and it's time for bed. My fall from the heights of my profession, my marriage and flight to America, my part in the hunt for President Lincoln's assassin, and the story of my passionate association with the most renowned actress of the day, famous in America and Europe—that must await another day.

You'll stay up a while? Ah, it's a fresh bottle of rum you're opening: tipple of the sailor, hey? Well, I must confess I'm more inclined to brandy and water myself, but now you insist, perhaps as a nightcap, I'll take one more small one with you. . . .

But one only, and then, to the arms of Lethe!

AFTERWORD

During his account of his life I felt occasional irritations at the exposure of Mr James's prejudices: for instance, Prince Albert was not *Prussian*. He was of the House of Saxe Coburg. And I confess that after hearing the story of my stepfather's rise to the heights of his profession, and the manner in which he achieved his seat at Marylebone I was taken with a certain degree of scepticism. However, on taking the trouble to check the public records I have become convinced that by and large Mr James was telling the truth. His professional relationship with Alexander Cockburn is well documented and Cockburn certainly defended James in the House when questions were raised as to his suitability to become a Recorder. His account of the 1847 Horsham by-election was also true: the election became a by-word for bribery and corruption and was regarded as scandalous even by the standards of the time. The part played by Mr James is also well documented, and his account largely accurate.

His personal escapades with Alexander Cockburn cannot be confirmed from public accounts, naturally enough. But they have the ring of truth. These were men of their times: Viscount Palmerston was noted for his amatory wandering in corridors late at night; Cockburn's unusual extra-marital escapades were as well known as those of Wilkie Collins, Charles Dickens and

Thackeray; and as for my stepfather's skills before a jury, they were much commented upon at the time. Comment was not always favourable: I recently came across a letter to *The Times*, for instance, published in 1857, where the writer complained that Mr James was *'notorious for his jocularity and indulges in it frequently at the expense of that delicacy, propriety and seriousness which should characterize the proceedings of a court of justice.'* The writer considered that the Court of Queen's Bench was not *'the proper scene for coarse ribaldry and insult to a lady'*. But the juries evidently liked it—and brought in verdicts for his clients.

As for oratory, Mr James's speech in defence of Dr Simon Bernard can be judged on its merits: it was published in pamphlet form and at the time lauded for its oratorical sweep. Similarly, his speeches in Parliament are a matter of record in *Hansard* so much of what he recounted to me can be taken as true. Moreover, he was remarkably frank with me about the reprehensible manner in which he and his leader, Attorney General Cockburn, conducted the Palmer prosecution: it gave rise to much criticism at the time, as Mr James mentioned, and was roundly condemned by senior members in the profession—though much of the blame was directed towards the Bench, and particularly towards the summing-up by Lord Chief Justice Campbell.

And yet there were some issues that left me with nagging doubts. The confession of Edward Agar to the court in 1855 made no mention of my stepfather; the death of Lord George Bentinck remained mysterious and much commented upon, but it was never suggested in the Press that it might have been murder—or that Mr James, or John Sadleir, was involved. But, so many years after the event, what reason would he have for lying about such matters to me? Particularly since they do not cast him in a favourable light. As for the startling revelation concerning John Sadleir's suicide, whatever the truth may be it must be a matter for remark that one rogue—my stepfather—was called upon to identify the corpse of an even bigger rogue! Coincidence, possibly. Or perhaps Mr James was telling me the truth.

Why would he, even after such a length of time, confide such secrets to me? One can conjecture, of course: it might have been pride, perhaps, or the need to impress me, or the desire to fantasize, spin tall tales—we hear many such on long voyages before the mast. And certainly there remained a nagging doubt in my mind as he talked, the thought that he might have been merely boasting, or seeking to make sense of his career, bring logic and reason to the events, assign blame and responsibility to others, eliminate— or emphasize—the part that chance played in his life.

What I certainly have to balance in the ledger is that his memory was certainly failing him when he gave his account to me. He was vague, even inaccurate about dates and timings, and that must raise some doubts about his revelations. For instance, a minor matter: the *Lord Huntingtower* case took place before, not after *Running Rein*. Again, the action in which he first met the Rugeley poisoner, Dr Palmer, was brought by a moneylender called Padwick, not Padstone, as Mr James identified him. More seriously, he seems to have conflated events in an odd fashion, confused and compressed them in timescale: the Derby case took place in 1844, Mr James took up residence at The Nunnery in 1845, the Horsham by-election occurred in 1847, the Palmer case in 1855. But Sir John Jervis died in 1850 and James was not appointed Queen's Counsel till 1854. The gold bullion robbery occurred in 1854, and Agar's trial in 1855. Mr James's appointment as Recorder to Brighton really took place in 1850, his election to Parliament was not won until 1859. But in his account to me these events seem to have been intermingled, made consequentially in a somewhat distorted sequence.

However, perhaps these discrepancies are to be explained by the fading faculties of an ageing man, the confused memory for dates and timings of events that took place decades earlier, the emotional need to bring order to the chaotic course of personal events. I may point to a similar problem to be found in the recently published memoirs of another lawyer, a contemporary of Mr James. William Ballantine's first published memoirs were widely read and this encouraged him to write a sequel. The second book was poorly received; it was obvious that in the interim period his memory had become confused and vague and uncertain so the second volume was virtually incomprehensible.

I am left with the knowledge that much of what Mr James told me can be confirmed from other sources, even though the more startling confessions, such as to the fates of Lord George Bentinck and John Sadleir MP must continue to remain veiled in mystery. Yet in the balance, I feel that what my stepfather related to me can be taken largely as truth.

And his account certainly has some value in that it confirms and explains events that have puzzled commentators over the ensuing years. And there yet remained the story of his adventures in Italy, with Garibaldi, and the startling story of his years in the United States, his involvement in the events surrounding the death of the President, his liaison with the most famous actress in America and Europe. . . . It was a narrative that I was anticipating with some eagerness, not least since it dealt with a period in which I myself was for a time living in New York, years when world-shattering events took place in which my stepfather apparently played a significant part.

Joachim Edgar Stocqueler
Master Mariner
1889